"You may kiss the bride."

Drew turned to Tia and their eyes met. His were dark and serious, clouded with something Tia now understood very well. Confusion. They had taken the biggest step a man and woman could take together. They had done it for some very good reasons. But if their fifteen-minute service had almost sucked her into believing this was real, how would she possibly survive eight months?

Drew bent his head and touched his lips to hers, but before he could pull away, Tia slid her right arm around his neck and nudged him to stay where he was. They wouldn't give the impression of two people so enamored they had to get married in two weeks with a peck on the cheek.

They had to really kiss.

Dear Reader,

After looking at winter's bleak landscape and feeling her icy cold breezes, I found nothing to be more rewarding than savoring the warm ocean breezes from a poolside lounge chair as I read a soon-to-be favorite book or two! Of course, as I choose my books for this long-anticipated outing, this month's Silhouette Romance offerings will be on the top of my pile.

Cara Colter begins the month with *Chasing Dreams* (#1818), part of her A FATHER'S WISH trilogy. In this poignant title, a beautiful academic moves outside her comfort zone and feels alive for the first time in the arms of a brawny man who would seem her polar opposite. When an unexpected night of passion results in a pregnancy, the hero and heroine learn that duty can bring its own sweet rewards, in *Wishing and Hoping* (#1819), the debut book in beloved series author Susan Meier's THE CUPID CAMPAIGN miniseries. Elizabeth Harbison sets out to discover whether bustling New York City will prove the setting for a modern-day fairy tale when an ordinary woman comes face-to-face with one of the world's most eligible royals, in *If the Slipper Fits* (#1820). Finally, Lissa Manley rounds out the month with *The Parent Trap* (#1821), in which two matchmaking girls set out to invent a family.

Be sure to return next month when Cara Colter concludes her heartwarming trilogy.

Happy reading!

Ann Leslie Tuttle
Associate Senior Editor

Please address questions and book requests to:
Silhouette Reader Service
U.S.: 3010 Walden Ave., P.O. Box 1325, Buffalo, NY 14269
Canadian: P.O. Box 609, Fort Erie, Ont. L2A 5X3

Wishing
AND
Hoping
SUSAN MEIER

The Cupid Campaign

SILHOUETTE *Romance*®

Published by Silhouette Books

America's Publisher of Contemporary Romance

SILHOUETTE BOOKS

ISBN 0-373-19819-1

WISHING AND HOPING

Copyright © 2006 by Linda Susan Meier

Visit Silhouette Books at www.eHarlequin.com

Printed in U.S.A.

SUSAN MEIER

is one of eleven children, and though she's yet to write a book about a big family, many of her books explore the dynamics of "unusual" family situations, such as large work "families," bosses who behave like overprotective fathers, or "sister" bonds created between friends. Because she has more than twenty nieces and nephews, children also are always popping up in her stories. Many of the funny scenes in her books are based on experiences raising her own children or interacting with her nieces and nephews. She was born and raised in western Pennsylvania and continues to live in Pennsylvania.

For my parents, whose continuing romance through their marriage showed me that love really can be everlasting.

Chapter One

"**I**'m pregnant."

Tia Capriotti stood on the porch of Drew Wallace's white French Colonial farmhouse, staring at the father of her child. His shiny black hair, usually hidden by his Stetson, was sexily disheveled and his dark eyes glittered sexily, but that was Drew. He was handsome. He was sexy. And she now knew he was out of her league.

The sounds of two stable hands leaving for the day alerted Tia to the fact that they might be overheard. She knew Drew realized that too when he grabbed her forearm and pulled her into his foyer, quickly closing the stained-glass door behind her.

"Say that again."

She raised her eyes to meet his gaze. "I'm pregnant."

"Oh, God!" was all Drew said as he sat down heavily

on the fourth step of the stairway. His butt hit the soft carpet runner as his boots thumped on the hardwood floor.

Tia said nothing, giving him time to get his bearings, remembering, as he probably was, the night they had run into each other at a party in Pittsburgh, Pennsylvania, so far away from Calhoun Corners, Virginia, that he'd never expected to come across somebody from his hometown. He'd always known her as Isabella. So when their host introduced her as Tia—a nickname she'd picked up in college—without her last name, he hadn't associated her with his formerly chubby, long-haired next-door neighbor, whom he hadn't seen since she'd left for college six years before.

But she had assumed he'd recognized her because he didn't ask her last name and flirted with her as if she were the love of his life—something she'd dreamt of through high school when she'd had a killer crush on him. She was thrilled when he'd accepted her invitation to come back to her house.

They hadn't caught the misunderstanding until after they'd made love, but when he had discovered she was Isabella Capriotti, not just plain Tia-somebody-or-another-who-worked-at-an-ad-firm-in-downtown-Pittsburgh, Drew had been furious. He'd felt she should have realized he hadn't recognized her, if only because she should have known he wouldn't have a one-night stand with the daughter of the man who had helped him build his horse-breeding business. And if that wasn't enough, he didn't sleep with women twelve years younger than he was.

After his outburst, Tia had stared at him mutely, thinking his understanding of romance was nonexistent. He had no qualms about jumping into bed with a total stranger, but he was upset about making love to *her*—mostly because he knew her.

Still, she had her pride. When they had made love, he'd believed she was somebody else. She couldn't even remotely pretend the man of her high-school fantasies loved her. And the way he had scolded her had made her blood boil. She was an adult. She had a job and a house. A bank had considered her responsible enough to give her a mortgage. She hadn't deserved to be treated like a little girl.

And that's exactly what she had told him before she'd asked him to leave. When he'd walked out her door that night she had been convinced that she would never see him again.

She knew he wouldn't be happy she was pregnant, but she was here to assure him he needn't be concerned. She might be twelve years younger than he was, but she was a twenty-four-year-old woman who made enough money to support a child. She was ready to become a mom. He could have as much or as little involvement with this baby as he wanted.

"Don't worry. I have everything under control."

"What about me? Don't I get any say in this?"

"I absolutely want you to be involved in our baby's life, but there's no pressure. You have the option to be as involved as you want to be."

He gaped at her. "That's your idea of having everything under control? To give me the 'option' of being involved in our baby's life?"

"No!" Tia said, baffled by how he had twisted everything. "I have a job and my own house…"

"I'm not talking about finances. I'm talking about the personal end of things. A child should have its father's name."

He sounded exactly as her dad sounded any time he heard of a woman having a baby on her own, and Tia realized that this was probably why women didn't date men too much older than they were.

"As far as I'm concerned the first thing we need to do is get married."

Tia's heart thumped at the possibility of being the wife of the man she'd fantasized about since she was fourteen. But she knew he didn't want to marry her. And she didn't think she wanted to marry him, either. Not after the way he'd reacted the night they'd made love. No thanks.

"I didn't come here to extort marriage from you. The baby can just take your name. It doesn't matter if we're married when he's born—"

"Maybe not to you, but it does to me and I'll bet it does to your dad." He paused and groaned. "Damn it! We have a bigger reason to get married than giving the baby my name."

Not quite sure she trusted him, Tia peered at him. "And that reason is?"

"Your dad's reelection campaign is in trouble."

"Really?" she asked dubiously. Her dad had been

mayor of Calhoun Corners since she was six. No one ever voted against him.

"For the first time in close to twenty years, your dad has an opponent. Auggie Malloy. His entire platform is based on the fact that your dad had a heart attack last year. Everybody knows he takes pills when he's stressed and Auggie's saying that makes him too sick to be mayor. And Mark Fegan agrees," Drew said, referring to the editor of the *Calhoun Corners Chronicle*. "He's been running editorials supporting Auggie."

This time it was Tia who groaned. "Are you kidding me? By doing that he's actually causing the stress that causes my dad's chest pain."

"And makes your dad look too weak to be mayor. But even so, the election isn't our problem. Our problem is that your dad has enough stress already and God only knows how he's going to react when we tell him I got you pregnant in a one-night stand and we're not getting married because we don't really know each other—but we had sex."

Tia fell to the step just below the one on which Drew sat. She hadn't intended to tell her dad the "circumstances" under which she got pregnant, but she understood what Drew was saying. With the stress her dad already had, there was a chance that any news that made him angry could be the stress that pushed him over the edge, and she didn't even want to put into words what would happen then.

"What if we don't tell him until after the election?"

"There are six months until the election. Do you

think you're not going to be showing any time in the next six months? Or that the stress of the election will lessen as we get closer to the day that everybody goes to the polls? If anything, the stress is going to increase. It's better to tell him you're pregnant now before the election stress is at its worst, when he really could have a heart attack."

As Tia tried to think it through, Drew scooted off his stair to pace the foyer, his boots making a thumping sound on the hardwood with every step. But he suddenly turned and stood towering over her. Because it was a hot June day, he wore only jeans and a T-shirt that his chest and broad shoulders stretched to capacity. His penetrating brown eyes seemed to be able to see the whole way to her soul. He was so attractive it almost hurt to look at him. She swallowed.

"This doesn't have to be complicated. If we tell your dad we've been secretly dating and you're pregnant so we're getting married, nobody will blink an eye. And it's not like we have to be 'really' married. You work in Pittsburgh. I live in Virginia. We don't even have to see each other except for a few weekends to make the situation look believable. We can divorce after the baby's born and once again I'll bet nobody will even blink an eye, if only because with you working in Pittsburgh and me living in Virginia everybody will say our marriage was doomed from the start."

What he said made a lot of sense. They could pretend to be married without having to live together because of her job. Plus, not seeing much of each other was a built-in explanation for why the marriage would fail. Oddly enough, it was the perfect way to hide the bad part of their situation while revealing the good parts. Her parents didn't have any grandchildren. A wedding and a baby right now might be a calming influence. At the very least, a baby and a wedding could make her parents happy.

"Okay. We'll get married."

"Okay."

The foyer became incredibly quiet. They spent the next few seconds staring at each other and it sunk in for Tia that she was marrying the guy she'd dreamed about from the day she'd met him when she was fourteen. Unfortunately, the wedding wasn't happening anywhere near the way she'd envisioned it. And, even more unfortunately, Drew Wallace wasn't the Prince Charming she had imagined in her teenage fantasies. In fact, he was pretty much the opposite of the sweet, sincere gentleman she had pictured him to be.

Drew suddenly turned and grabbed his Stetson from a peg by the door. "Let's go tell your parents."

Her gaze jerked back to his. "Now?"

"If we don't do this now, we're both going to lose courage. Or we'll try to talk ourselves out of it. Trust me. When it comes to ugly situations like this, I know exactly how to get out of them."

A quiver of misgiving shuddered through Tia. She wasn't so naive as to think that a man as handsome and sexy as Drew got to be thirty-six without being involved with other women. Maybe even lots of women. But she'd never thought of him as needing to "get out of things." Worse, she'd never thought far enough ahead to consider that he might actually be involved with somebody right now.

She rose from the step. "I'm not about to be confronted by an angry woman for stealing her man, am I?"

With his hand already on the doorknob, Drew let out a gust of air and faced her. "You're not stealing anybody's man."

"Because you don't have somebody?"

"Because we're not staying married."

"So this marriage won't even be a bump in the road for you?"

Drew looked at her as if she were crazy and she said, "Never mind." She stepped out onto the porch ahead of him and ran down the steps to the sidewalk, knowing that for the next several months, maybe even year, she was stuck with the grumpiest man on the face of the earth. "This is going to be fun."

"It doesn't have to be fun. It doesn't have to be much of anything since we only have to spend enough time together that your parents don't suspect the marriage is fake."

"As I said, sounds like a barrel of fun."

After crunching across the gravel to the big black truck he had parked in front of his garage, Drew opened the door to the cab and gestured for Tia to climb inside. "And as I said, it doesn't need to be fun. Only official."

Tia walked past him. She was pregnant with his baby and had conspired to enter into a fake marriage with him, yet he was barking orders as if he still saw her as a child.

"I'll take my own car, thanks," she said, her voice prim and proper. "There's no reason for me to drive back here just to pick it up."

He slammed the truck door. "Good point."

"Whatever," she said, and marched to her little red sports car.

She got inside, closed her door with enough force to rattle the windows and had her vehicle roaring down the lane toward the main highway before Drew turned to walk to the driver's-side door.

Anger ricocheted through Drew. He kicked both front tires of his truck on his way around each fender and slammed his door, too.

His only consolation was that he knew Tia wasn't really driving too fast. Her sports car had a big engine that would roar anytime anyone hit the gas even slightly. But occupying his brain with anger about her driving was much better than thinking about telling his mentor and friend that his daughter was about to have a baby. *His* baby....

Drew paused and, dropping his head, let his forehead bump against the steering wheel. *His baby.*

Dear God. He was going to be a father.

Even as the thought filled him with an emotion that made his heart feel as if it was surrounded by warm oatmeal, it also struck pure terror in that same heart. Not because he thought he couldn't handle being a dad, but because he knew he could *not* handle being married. One incredibly ugly divorce had taught him that lesson. His ex-wife had bled him dry. But that wasn't the worst.

The worst was discovering, after he'd literally sold his share of his first business to his partner to pay her settlement, that she just happened to be having an affair with that same partner.

Drew squeezed his eyes shut, angry with himself for thinking of things so far in the past, but he couldn't stop the memories. Sandy hadn't been his first love. He'd had girlfriends, been in love, and even lived with someone for a few months before he'd met Sandy, so he wasn't naive. But Sandy had been special. She was funny, interesting, smart and one of the most wonderful women he had ever met. He remembered some nights just watching her sleep, totally grateful that she was his.

Her request for a divorce had come out of the blue and had blindsided him. When he had opened the envelope from the process server he was sure he and his partner were being sued by one of their contractors. That would have been stunning enough. But to see in print Sandy's name and his name and the word *divorce* on the same page, when he hadn't even known there was trouble in paradise, had paralyzed him.

Figuring that it might be a joke or a mistake, he had raced home to talk to Sandy, but she had coldly assured him that it was neither a mistake nor a joke. He had begged her to let him make it up to her—though he hadn't really understood what he'd done wrong. She had handed him a suitcase, told him she was changing the locks and escorted him to the door.

And he'd stood there. On the front stoop of the brand-new house they were supposed to share. Probably for a half hour. Numb and confused.

After the divorce, he had wished he'd stayed numb. Because when he had learned his wife had kicked him out so she could marry his former partner, he had gotten so angry he'd punched Mac Franklin. That cost him a night in jail.

But even that wasn't the worst. The worst had been loving somebody who didn't love him. The worst had been living in the same town when the woman he loved and the partner he admired got engaged, then married. The worst had been looking at her happy pictures in the newspaper and wondering where the hell he had gone wrong. Wondering why she had fallen out of love, and when. Wondering what was wrong with him that she didn't want him. Going over every second of their two years together that he could remember and coming up empty. Feeling he hadn't done anything wrong and wishing, almost begging God to let him have done something—even something small—so he would know not to do it again. So he'd have some hope for the future.

But that mythical "thing" he might have done never materialized. He was the victim, the guy who had been wronged, yet he was still the one who had lost everything. And maybe that was the reason the whole deal never really settled itself for him. There was no lesson to be learned except that he wouldn't ever trust anybody with so much of his life again.

And Isabella—Tia—had already tricked him.

Not intentionally, Drew reminded himself. As she'd

told him after they had made love, she'd lost weight and cut her long brown hair immediately after she had graduated from college. It was her first step in trying to get people to see her as more mature, but Drew didn't know that. Because she didn't look like the Isabella who had gone off to college, and because she had been introduced as Tia, and because they were so far away from home that he wasn't thinking about anybody from Calhoun Corners, let alone somebody he hadn't seen in six years, he had never suspected she was his former neighbor.

The whole situation was a jumble of confusion, but it was a manageable jumble. What wasn't manageable—or predictable or even something he wanted—was a long-term involvement with a woman. But just because he and Tia were parents, that didn't necessarily mean they had to be "involved." If he could endure being married for eight short months, all he had to worry about were the times he dropped off or picked up their child. And as he'd already pointed out to Tia, she lived in Pittsburgh. At best, throughout this marriage they'd see each other on weekends.

Everything would be fine.

He drove down her parents' tree-lined lane, very much like his own, to the Capriotti horse farm. His house was a white French Colonial, built as a gift to himself for finally succeeding financially the way he had always known he could, but Tia's parents lived in a redbrick farmhouse that had been updated and renovated several times. Long and regal, it somehow managed to look more like a home than any house Drew had ever seen.

But even as the site comforted him, Drew's stomach knotted. Ben Capriotti had saved his sanity. After losing his half of the architectural firm to his wife, Drew wasn't going into architecture again because he was sure that profession was bad luck for him. When he had explained that to Ben, Ben had laughed and agreed to teach Drew everything he needed to know about breeding horses, and getting involved in something so complex hadn't left Drew time to think about his ex-wife or his ex-partner. Ben had kept his promise and helped Drew every step along the way, and Drew had repaid him by getting his only daughter pregnant.

If he could take one thing back in his life, it would be making love to Tia that night in May. But since he couldn't, he would at least do the right thing.

He shoved open his truck door and joined Tia on the front porch. Apparently over her anger with him, or maybe because she knew they needed to present a unified front to her parents, she quietly said, "Ready?"

Without hesitation or thought, he took her hand and caught her gaze. Bad move. The combination of those pretty blue eyes and the smoothness of her skin shot arousal through him. But Tia didn't seem to have the same problem. She didn't gasp or shiver. Her eyes didn't darken with desire or even simple awareness. Instead, her expression grew puzzled.

Thanks. That was great for the ego.

He sighed and raised their joined hands. "If we're going to get away with this lie, there are a couple of things we'll have to do."

He tried to ignore the electricity sizzling between their clasped hands, but he couldn't. Though it had been more than a month since they'd been together, the heat they had generated that night was alive and well and giving him the kinds of thoughts that could get a man arrested in some states, reminding him of something he'd forgotten to even consider. How the hell did he expect to be married to this woman without sleeping with her?

Through sheer force of will. Tia was the only daughter of his mentor, which meant Drew had only one real concern. Making sure he didn't push Ben Capriotti over the edge of his stress limit. To do that Drew only had to *pretend* to like Tia. He did not actually have to like her. When it came to common sense and sheer force of will, Drew knew he was the best. There would be no problem with his self-control.

"Holding hands is the easiest way to immediately clue them in that we're more than friends."

When Tia's tongue came out to moisten her lips and she gazed into his eyes for a few seconds too long, Drew almost groaned. Not because the sexy gesture reminded him of just how difficult ignoring her was going to be, but because the lip-moistening demonstrated that she wasn't nearly as unaffected as he had thought.

Well, whatever. He hadn't met a woman he couldn't cause to dislike him. Even Tia had kicked him out of her house the night they'd made love. In a few weeks he could have her absolutely hating him. And he would. Right after they convinced her parents they were crazy in love and getting married.

"Don't take anything I say in here personally," he said, then turned and opened the front door, leading her into her parents' house.

When they entered the foyer, Tia called, "Mom? Dad?"

"In the den, honey," her mother answered. "Come on back."

"Okay," Tia said casually, but Drew's stomach plummeted. He considered giving himself a minute to calm down, but knew things weren't going to get any better with the passage of time, so they might as well get this over with.

"Let's go."

With a slight tug on Tia's hand, he led her into her father's den. Her parents were seated together on the old tan leather sofa, reviewing the records for the farm.

As they entered the den, her mother glanced up. Drew knew Tia had gotten her size and shape from her mother, an average-height brunette with pretty green eyes. But her dark brown hair and blue eyes came from her dad.

"Drew?" Elizabeth Capriotti's gaze skittered over to Tia, then unerringly honed in on their joined hands. "Tia?"

"Hi, Mom," Tia said, then—probably because she was as nervous as he was—she unexpectedly blurted, "Drew and I are getting married."

Her dad put down the computer printout he was holding. Looking totally baffled, he rose. "What did you say?"

"We're getting married," Drew said, squeezing Tia's hand and hoping she got the message to let him handle this. "Tia wasn't supposed to just drop that bomb on you like that."

Her dad took two steps toward them. "How exactly would you suggest my daughter…my *only* daughter…my *baby* daughter…tell me that she's about to marry a man who is ten…no, *twelve*…years older than she is?"

"I know this looks bad," Tia began, but Drew lightly squeezed her hand again, reminding her to let him be the one to speak. Their whole purpose in getting married was to downplay the problem, and Drew was an expert at that.

"Ben, the news Tia and I have gets worse before it gets better. Since she started the ball rolling by blurting out that we're getting married, I'm going to put all our cards on the table and tell you she's pregnant."

Tia's dad gasped, stumbled then clutched his chest. Tia cried, "Dad!" snatched her hand back from Drew and rushed to her father.

"Ben!" Elizabeth shouted, jumping from her seat and running to the big mahogany desk to grab her husband's pills.

But Ben waved Tia away as he turned to call his wife back. "Don't, Elizabeth. I'm fine. But you two really are getting married," he said, turning back to Drew and Tia. "And this pregnancy stays a secret until after the election. I'm contending with enough right now without adding the gossip of your shenanigans to the mix. Understood?"

Drew said, "Understood," as Tia simultaneously said, "I understand."

Ben shook his head. "No, you don't understand, Tia.

You live in Pittsburgh. You haven't been reading the paper, seeing how Mark Fegan's keeping conversation focused on my damn heart condition so Auggie Malloy doesn't have to deal with real issues—" He waved his hand. "Hell. Forget it. The campaign's my problem. I'll handle it." He pointed a stern finger at Tia and Drew. "But you two get married, and I mean right now."

With that he returned to the sofa, sat and began going through the bills on the coffee table, dismissing Tia and Drew. Elizabeth hurriedly motioned for Tia and Drew to follow her out of the room.

As she closed the den door she said, "We didn't even know you were dating."

"We didn't date long," Drew said, silently congratulating himself for his cleverness. He hadn't lied, but he also hadn't admitted that they'd had a one-night stand.

"And we *are* happy," Tia said.

Knowing that wasn't at all true, Drew could only guess Tia had said that because it was the one thing her mother wouldn't argue about. Elizabeth might be upset about her daughter marrying someone older, but she wouldn't argue with her little girl's happiness. He gave Tia points for recognizing that and decided that maybe, between the two of them, this wouldn't be *too* godawful difficult to pull off, after all.

"Do you think Daddy's okay?" Tia asked softly.

Elizabeth nodded. "He's fine. Parents deal with unexpected babies and weddings every day of the week." She blew her breath out on a long sigh. "It's the election that's making him nuts."

"We're sorry that this comes at such a bad time," Tia said.

"When do you plan to get married?"

Drew said, "I thought we'd just get a license and go see a judge…"

Elizabeth's eyes rounded with sorrow. "No wedding?"

"Sorry, Elizabeth," Drew said, "but we're a little pressed for time. As Ben said, we won't announce that Tia's pregnant for a few months, but the quicker we get married, the better."

"I could put something together in two weeks," Elizabeth insisted. "That would be the first of July. You could get married in the gazebo in the backyard and we could have a small reception under a tent." She gazed at Drew imploringly. "It wouldn't be any trouble."

"Elizabeth—" Drew began.

But Tia interrupted him. "I think that's a great idea, Mom. A wedding will be something fun for all of us. Maybe give Dad a break from the election for a day. As long as we keep it to a little wedding in the backyard."

"That's perfect," Elizabeth said. "Nothing fancy. Just something small."

Tia turned to Drew. "Unless you want to help Mom and me make wedding plans, you can go now."

It took a second before Drew understood she was telling him his work here was done. When he got it, everything inside him melted with relief and he said, "Okay. I'll see you tomorrow."

"Tomorrow?" Elizabeth echoed. "You're leaving?"

"I'm not much on girlie stuff, Elizabeth."

Elizabeth looked at Tia. "But *you're* staying?"

"To help you plan—"

"All night?" Elizabeth said, but as she spoke her puzzled expression changed to a shrewd-mother smile. "Tia? What's going on here?"

Chapter Two

"Nothing's going on!" Drew said, grabbing Tia by the shoulders and turning her in the direction of the foyer. Tia struggled against his hold, but he gripped her tighter.

"Tia forgot how late it was when she volunteered to help plan tonight. You go back to the den and check on Ben. You can call us tomorrow morning and we'll come over and talk about wedding plans then. Or Tia can come over by herself…whatever you and Ben want."

With that, Drew pushed Tia up the hall and she gave up fighting him because it wasn't good for her mother to see them argue or question each other.

But when they were on the front porch, out of range of both of her parents, she glared at him. "Drew—"

"Shhh," he said, pulling her down the steps and all but dragging her to her car. "If we don't make too much of a ruckus, maybe nobody will notice we brought two vehicles."

He tucked her inside her little red sports car, then raced over to his truck. Tia followed him back to his house. Not at all happy with his high-handedness, she parked her car beside his in front of the two-car garage, walked into the foyer and tossed her car keys onto the curio cabinet.

"If you'd given me two minutes I could have talked my mother into planning tonight and I wouldn't have had to come back here!"

"That was exactly the problem," Drew said as he ambled off to the left into his living room. "It was obvious that you were trying to get rid of me when we're supposed to be madly in love and you're supposed to *want* to spend the night with me."

Still in the foyer, Tia froze by the stairway. She barely had time to register a grateful reaction for his saving their charade. The words *spend the night with me* caused her chest to tighten and her pulse to scramble. She sure as heck hoped he didn't think they should be sharing the same bed, but even as the idea entered her brain she knew that's exactly what he thought. She was already pregnant. He knew she found him attractive. They had been magnificent together sexually. Plus, they were getting married. They would be each other's opposite-sex companion for the next eight months. She couldn't envision him going without sex for eight months.

She leaned against the newel post to steady herself. This situation just kept getting worse.

Well, she'd already faced two awkward conversations this evening. Time for number three.

Straightening her shoulders, she headed for his living room.

Seated on a white brocade sofa, with his arms stretched across its back and his boots on the coffee table, Drew looked disreputable and self-assured and so handsome that Tia had a sudden case of second thoughts. They might not be right for each other as a real husband and wife, but would sleeping together for the next eight months really be that bad?

"Your mother is suspicious," Drew said, "because our story is weak. Not only do we have to come up with a more detailed story than what we told your parents, but we should also have a prenup."

Tia's eyes widened and her mouth fell open slightly. "You don't have to protect your money from me!"

"How do you know I wasn't trying to protect *your* money from *me?*"

Taken aback by that possibility, she thought about it, then remembered she didn't have any money to protect. She'd only been working two years. Not enough time to accumulate a nest egg. Any money she had saved had gone into the down payment for her house.

"I don't have any money."

"Okay, then we're back to protecting mine. But for a few seconds there, when you thought you might have money, you have to admit you wanted a prenup, too."

This was why she wouldn't sleep with him. He was nothing like the guy of her childhood fantasies. He wasn't a sweet, considerate, smitten Prince Charming. He was a grouch who perpetually watched out for himself. "You're insane."

"Frankly, my dear, I don't care what you think of me." He pushed himself off the sofa and poured two fingers of Scotch. "Can I get you something? Soda? Iced tea? Glass of milk?"

"I'm fine," she said, but she wasn't. This morning she had been a happy-go-lucky employee at an advertising firm. She had a job secure enough that she was ready, even happy, to become a mom. In her generosity of spirit and fairness of heart, she'd decided to tell her baby's father he was about to be a dad. She'd agreed to marry him to protect her father from the potential stress that telling the real story might generate. Now, her father was okay, but she was stuck spending too much time with a man who always looked on the dark side of things. She wished she had realized Drew wasn't the nice guy she had created in her fantasies before she'd made love with him, but she'd been so caught up in her childhood crush that she'd let herself believe he was the man in her dreams.

He wasn't. She didn't know exactly who he was, but he most certainly wasn't Prince Charming.

"I'm not sleeping with you."

He peered at her over his Scotch glass. His gaze went from her short cap of dark hair, along her face, down her shoulders, pausing at her breasts, and then tumbled to her toes. For a few seconds he appeared to be considering his answer. Finally, he smiled and said, "I don't remember asking."

Embarrassment shot through her, but she ignored it. She didn't believe for one second that he didn't want to sleep with her. Still, she wasn't arguing with good fortune.

"Let's just say that was another one of those things we had to get out of the way."

"Good."

"Good."

He strolled back to the white sofa and settled again on the plump cushion. "Let's get back to the prenup."

"I don't have any money. I don't want yours. I think your lawyer should be able to handle that."

"You don't want your lawyer to draw it up?"

"I don't have a lawyer."

"Then we'll use mine. But you should get one to look it over before you sign it."

"Why? Planning to cheat me?"

"No, just teaching you to watch your back. Marriage is as much a business proposition as anything else. It pays not to forget that."

She would have had a snappy comeback, but as he spoke the room began to spin. She swayed slightly and groped for the back of a nearby club chair with cognac-colored pillows that matched the silk printed drapes.

Before she had a solid hold, Drew was at her side. "Whoa. Are you okay?"

"Yeah, I'm fine. But it's been a long day." Really long. All she had wanted was to do the right thing. For her trouble, she was stuck with a lunatic arguing about prenups. "I'm exhausted."

"Then we'll talk in the morning. We have the whole house to ourselves for at least two weeks because my housekeeper is taking care of her sister in Minneapolis after surgery. We don't have to figure everything out tonight."

Tia shifted out from under his hold. "Great. I'll get my overnight bag from my car, then you can show me where to sleep."

"*I'll* get your overnight bag," Drew said as he caught her by the shoulders, turned her around and led her into the foyer. He pointed up the steps. "Pick any room you want. Just don't take the room at the end of the hall. That's mine. I'd give it to you if you insist, but since Mrs. Hernandez has been gone, it's a mess. The others are all clean. Take one of them." With that, he turned and walked out the front door.

Tia climbed the steps. At the top she gazed down the long, quiet corridor of the second floor of his brand-new house and counted six bedroom doors. She would have taken the first, but curiosity got the better of her and she sneaked down the hall, peeking into each room, gasping every time she opened a door because all six were beautifully appointed. Probably professionally decorated.

And she suddenly realized why Drew wanted a prenup. In the same way that she'd grown up in the past six years, he'd become wealthy. Maybe even the object of women pursuing him for his money. And she'd shown up on his doorstep waving the oldest trick in the book. A pregnancy. After a case of mistaken identity.

Wow. No wonder Drew wanted a prenup. For all practical intents and purposes, it looked as if she'd tricked him.

"Do you have any rope?"

Drew glanced up from reading the morning paper. When he saw Tia standing in his kitchen doorway, he steeled himself against the slam of desire that hit him like a tsunami. He didn't mind that she had the waistband of her too-big sweatpants bunched in her fist. What got to him was the enticing strip of belly flesh exposed because she had her white T-shirt tied at her midriff. It reminded him that he knew how soft she was. He knew how sweet she smelled. He knew just how good they had been together before he'd figured out she was Ben's daughter.

Which was exactly why she was totally off-limits. She was Ben's daughter. Not somebody he'd normally seduce. Not somebody he would sleep with again. Not only that, but their situation hadn't really been settled. If she wouldn't sign a prenup, he couldn't marry her.

When she'd conveniently become sick before they could finish their discussion about the prenup, it had finally sunk into Drew's thick skull that it was pretty darned odd that Tia had had absolutely no hesitation about making love the day they'd met at the party in Pittsburgh. They didn't really know each other as adults, so Drew knew there was no emotional bond between them. Which meant the most logical conclusion to be drawn for why she'd fall into the arms of a man she hardly knew was that she had wanted something.

He didn't have a clue what it was, but he did know that though he was duty-bound to raise his child and protect Ben, there was no way in hell he was losing half this farm. If she thought she was going to hoodwink him out of money, she was sadly mistaken. In fact, he'd decided not to push the issue of the prenup until he had a better handle on what game she was playing.

Gripping her too-big bottoms, Tia ambled to the table. "The first two weeks I was pregnant, I threw up every day and I lost ten pounds. Now all of my baggy clothes are way too baggy."

"There's plenty of rope for those pants in the stable," he said, and turned his attention back to his newspaper. "If we were staying for breakfast I'd get you a bale. Since we're going out, you might as well shower and put on something that fits."

"We're going out?"

"We need to be seen in public before your mother calls the preacher to arrange the ceremony or the local caterer to order two roasters of chicken for a buffet supper, and word of our marriage gets out."

"You're right."

"So go change and I'll see you at the truck."

Though Tia cringed at the mention of his truck, much to Drew's relief, she didn't argue. She left the kitchen and twenty minutes later, dressed in comfortable-looking capri pants and a crisp white blouse, she joined him by his black truck where he was talking over the day's chores with two hands.

"Jim, Pete," he said when Tia joined them. He slid his arm across her shoulders. "You remember Tia Capriotti, Ben's daughter."

Jim grinned. Pete took off his hat.

"Sure."

Tia extended her hand to shake both of theirs. "It's nice to meet you."

"We're going for breakfast right now," Drew said, not giving anybody a chance to really get to know each other. If her goal was to cheat him, he had to be very careful how chummy he let her get with the people close to him. He still had to marry her. He still wanted to be part of his child's life. But he'd be darned if he'd let her insinuate herself into his world enough that she could get information to use against him to take half of the farm he'd worked for for the past ten years. "We should be back at about eleven. I'll check on you then."

Jim and Pete nodded and headed for the stable. Drew turned Tia in the direction of his truck.

"How about if we take my car?"

"No."

"I no longer get morning sickness, but I still get motion sickness in any vehicle but my own car. We don't want to show up at the diner first thing in the morning with me green and begging for crackers."

He sighed. Unfortunately, she had a point. "Fine. But I'm driving."

Tia rolled her eyes. "I'm pregnant. I'm not an invalid."

"No, but I've seen the way you drive," he said, taking the keys from her. "I want to get there in one piece."

He opened the passenger's-side door for her. She got in and he closed the door, then rounded the hood. He slid into the driver's seat and started the engine. It purred to life like the finely tuned piece of engineering that it was, and he smiled. He didn't know a man in the world who wouldn't have smiled.

"Nice car." And not the car of a woman who needed to cheat a man out of money. He frowned. That really was the truth. This wasn't the car of a woman who needed to trick a man for money.

"Thanks. I bought it as a present to myself two years ago when I graduated."

Ah. Graduation money. The car didn't count. "What is it you do for a living, again?"

"I work for an ad firm."

"You took all those brains your dad told me you had and decided they would best serve the world by selling panty hose?"

She laughed. "I'm pretty good with panty hose, breakfast cereal is the specialty of the company I work for."

"You think hawking cereal is more important than science or medicine?"

"No, but I don't have a science or medicine kind of brain. I'm analytical, but I'm more verbal. I could have probably made a lot more money at a drug company, but I like what I do." She shrugged. "And I don't do so bad in the money department, either. In fact, as I climb the corporate ladder, my salary will increase quite nicely."

Drew frowned again. She sounded like a woman who had her future all planned out, not a woman who would marry a guy for money. But that only baffled him all the more. If she didn't want his money, what the hell did she want badly enough to make love with him that night in Pittsburgh?

"So you have a good job?"

She nodded. "And a house."

That's right! He'd been to her house. "Which means you should want a prenup as much as I do."

"Because of my house?" she laughed. "Every cent I had saved went into a down payment, and I mortgaged the rest. If you tried to take my house, I'd hand you the payment book."

"So you need money?"

She shook her head as if disgusted with him. "How many times do I have to tell you that I have a job. A good job. A job where I can climb the ladder. I have as much of a chance of being an executive at my company as anybody. I'm fine."

Drew shifted uncomfortably on the driver's seat of her car. He got it. She was self-sufficient. She didn't need him or his money. But that meant the only logical conclusion he could draw for why they'd ended up in bed was that she had been overwhelmingly attracted to him. So attracted to him she'd forgotten all about birth control. So attracted she'd fallen for stupid lines. Really fallen. She'd all but purred with happiness in his arms.

He swallowed, suddenly aware of how close they were in the confines of her tiny car. The attraction they'd felt the night they'd met at the party had not been one-sided. He'd been overwhelmingly attracted to her, too. On top of that, the heavenly soft, incredibly sensual woman beside him would be spending the next eight months of weekends with him. If he didn't get ahold of himself right now, all he would be thinking about for all eight of those months would be sex.

He parked her car in the lot beside the diner and guided her into the small restaurant. Filled with Saturday-morning patrons, the place was alive with conversation and brimming with the scents of fresh coffee, bacon and maple syrup.

"Good morning, Drew," Elaine Johnston said. Tall and amply built, the wife of Bill Johnston, the diner's owner, served as hostess normally, but also filled in as a waitress or cook. "And good morning to you, too, Isabella."

"She goes by Tia now," Drew interjected, and though Tia laughed, Drew was struck by what a smart move that had been. By telling Elaine that Tia no longed used Isabella but went by the name Tia, he subtly told the woman in contact with nearly everybody in Calhoun Corners that he knew personal things about Isabella Capriotti.

But though that was good for the charade, Drew felt an odd sensation in his gut. They were sexually attracted. She hadn't tricked him. She didn't need him. Hell, she didn't want him—except sexually. Now that he'd waded through the situation and realized she'd found him as irresistible as he'd found her, he was also recognizing that if he played his cards right she could want him again. And again. And again.

As Elaine led them down the aisle between two rows of booths, Drew inhaled a sharp breath. He had to stop thinking like this.

When they were seated and Elaine was on her way to get their coffee, Tia said, "So what now?"

His answer was quick and automatic. "We continue to make people believe that we are madly in love." But as the words came tumbling out of his mouth, he realized that if she wasn't the problem—if she hadn't tricked him and didn't want anything from him—then, technically, *he* was the problem. He'd seduced her. He was forcing her to marry him. He was demanding a place in her baby's life. And now he was thinking about seducing her again.

He was scum.

"We have to make people believe we're madly in love immediately? Can't we date?"

"We don't have time. Wedding's already set for two weeks from now. Besides, if we start here, right now, the rumor will get to Rayne Fegan this morning."

"Mark's daughter? What does she have to do with this?"

"Your dad's heart condition isn't the only thing in the editorials. Mark's also written about things your brothers did as teenagers, wondering why they were never arrested and almost accusing your dad of using influence to keep them out of jail."

"Are you kidding?"

"Mark's writing the editorials, but Rayne is the one digging up the past. We want her to find out we're together so she'll check up on us and decide we're for real, and let us alone."

"You've really thought this through."

"It's only common sense. There was no reason for Rayne to check on your brothers except to stress out your dad. When she hears about us she'll think she struck pay dirt for more ways to push your dad and she'll come gunning for us. But that's what we want. We want her to 'accidentally' find us looking calm and ordinary. Like this has been going on so long that we're comfortable. So nobody questions the wedding and there's nothing about it that stresses your dad."

Tia nodded, then leaned back and smiled at him. Once again, the easy upward movement of her lips was very good for the charade. Very bad for Drew's libido. Still, he knew what he had to do. Especially when he saw Ossie Burton striding toward them, an evil look on his face, as if he was about to have one hell of a time teasing Drew.

Drew's chest tightened. He'd vowed in every bar from here to the Chesapeake Bay that he'd never seriously date a woman again, let alone get married. He was not only about to endure months of the greatest physical challenge of his life by resisting a sexual attraction that suddenly seemed as natural as breathing, but he was also about to endure months of the teasing of his life.

Nonetheless, for Ben's sake, he reached across the table and took Tia's hand.

* * *

Tia and Drew ate breakfast interrupted by diner patrons who popped over to say hello, and the curious stares of people not bold enough to actually come over. When they left the diner, they walked to the small grocery store and picked up a few everyday items, making sure everybody saw them doing common, ordinary things. But when they reached the flower shop, Tia saw Rayne Fegan striding toward them.

"I told you she would track us down," Drew whispered as he put his hand on the doorknob to go inside. Rayne stopped them.

"Tia!" she said, catching Tia's arm to keep her from entering the flower shop. "My goodness, I didn't know you were home!"

"I've been home a few times since May." As if she'd done it a million times before, she turned and smiled at Drew.

Rayne's eyebrows rose. "Oh."

"We've been dating, Miss Nosey," Drew said. Compared to Tia, Rayne looked like somebody's maiden aunt. Though she wore her hair in a youthful ponytail, her long bangs sloppily brushed the frames of her outdated, oversize glasses. Her too-big blouse billowed over jeans that could have been taken in four inches. "I'll spell it out for you so you don't have to speculate in the newspaper."

"Very funny."

"It's not funny the way you're trying to take attention off the real issues of the election by focusing on Ben's health."

"He's our elected official. He set himself up to have his life scrutinized. Whether or not he can actually do the job is a part of that."

"He's done the job for an entire year since his heart attack," Tia said, joining Drew in defense of her father. "If you or your dad don't realize he's perfectly able to keep going then you're wrong."

"We don't think we are," Rayne said. "We think the town needs a young, enthusiastic mayor and we take the responsibility of the press very seriously."

"In other words," Drew countered, "you love making mountains out of molehills."

Rayne shook her head. "We're doing what needs to be done. Anytime he wants, Ben can pull out. From our point of view he's the one who needs to reevaluate." She sighed and glanced at Tia. Drew noticed the way her face softened with regret as she said, "It was nice to see you." Then she walked away.

"I get the feeling you and Rayne were friends at some point."

"We were two outcasts in high school. I was the brainy girl, she was the daughter of the guy who could put your misdeeds in the paper. We were a natural pair."

She turned and entered the flower shop. Drew followed her, putting his hand on the small of her back, directing her to the counter.

"What can I do for you, Tia, Drew?" Sam Jeffries said, wiping his hands on a white cloth as he approached from the table behind the counter where he had been arranging a huge funeral bouquet.

"We're getting married in two weeks," Drew said easily.

Sam grinned. "Well, that's a surprise."

Drew only smiled before he said, "Tia's mom will be handling most of the details, but Tia wanted to take a look around first so she knows what to tell her mother to order."

"I have catalogues," Sam said, not missing a beat. "I've got everything in here from altar bouquets to the bouquet the bride tosses when she leaves the reception."

"It's not going to be much of a reception," Tia said, taking her cue from Drew and speaking easily, naturally. "Just something small in my parents' backyard."

Sam flipped open a huge book. "Let me suggest you sift through these," he said, pointing at some pictures. "Match what you want as centerpieces or decorations with the flowers in your mother's gardens and it will be perfect."

Tia agreed with Sam's logic, but a strange feeling overwhelmed her as she glanced at the bouquets being held by the brides in the photos. Up until she actually saw these pictures, the wedding was an abstract thing. Planning not to live together except on weekends reinforced that. But knowing there would be a ceremony, that they were taking vows, buying flowers, made it all seem too real.

She was quiet on the drive home, but so was Drew. His face drawn in serious lines, he appeared to be thinking so intently about something that Tia knew he probably wouldn't hear her if she tried to make conversation. She let her gaze slide down to the sure way he gripped her steering wheel, then to his long legs. If she had thought her car was filled with him on the drive into town, it was even worse now.

Over and over she told herself that the awareness thrumming through her was purely sexual, but she couldn't help remembering that he was marrying her to protect her dad, his mentor. For as much as he'd tried to make her believe he was a jerk, she kept seeing that he had a soft side and she wished she wouldn't. Every time she realized how much he was putting himself out for her father, she started seeing the Prince Charming in him again and she didn't want to. She wanted that to be a lie. A sham. Her own imagination. She did not want him to be nice. She most certainly didn't want to like him. He'd made himself very clear the day before when he'd told her theirs would not be a real marriage. If she liked him too much, she would end up getting hurt.

She was glad he made the excuse of needing to check in with his hands, and left her to her own devices. She didn't even care when she saw him get into his truck and drive off. She jumped in her car and drove to her mother's, where she spent two hours deciding everything from what color her two cousins should wear as bridesmaids to which of their friends and neighbors should be invited.

When she returned to Drew's house to find it was still empty and there were no messages on his answering machine telling her where he was or when she could expect him back, she told herself she was grateful for his rudeness. It reminded her that he could be a real jerk.

But when another four hours passed without a word from him, that gratitude turned into absolute fury. The idiot had left her alone in his house. A house she didn't feel at liberty to explore now that she knew he had money. She didn't know where he was or what he was doing. If he had been in an accident, she didn't even know to send somebody out searching for him.

When he finally arrived home, she was waiting at the door. "Where were you?"

He bestowed upon her the sort of patient male look that all but locked in her perception that he was a total idiot. "What makes you think I'm supposed to check in with you?"

"I didn't ask you to check in with me. I'm a guest and you left me without a word. I had no idea where you were. So after I spent two hours planning our wedding with my mother, I sat here waiting for you, and I'm starving."

"You should have just eaten without me."

Shooting him daggers with her eyes, she turned and strode into the kitchen. "Very nice of you to tell me *now* that I can make myself to home."

"I thought that went without saying, since we're getting married." He followed her through the swinging door into the kitchen. "I have the prenup."

Tia stopped. *The prenup.* So that's where he was. Getting the document that put an end to all the worry she had that he might think she was trying to trick him. Once she signed it, he would recognize she didn't want his money. And she wouldn't have to walk on eggshells around him anymore.

"Great." Tia walked to the refrigerator, extracted a bag of rolls and a package of deli meat and took them to the table where he sat. "Where do I sign?"

He handed her the agreement. "Last page."

"Got a pen?"

"Aren't you going to read it?"

"Should I?"

"Yes." His voice was quiet, not at all grouchy or demanding, and she suddenly knew what was going on. Pragmatic Drew wanted her to see *he* wasn't cheating *her.* If nothing else, she always had to give this guy credit for fairness and common sense. Only an idiot signed a legal document without reading it.

"You're right."

After making a sandwich, she sat at the table and quickly scanned the agreement, reading exactly what she expected to read: articles that outlined that they would each keep the property that they had when they came into the marriage and not have a claim to anything owned by the other. It was short and simple and Tia almost stopped reading, but the very last paragraph shifted in tone.

She read the article and slammed the prenup on the table. "Very funny."

"I didn't put any jokes in there. So you're going to have to explain which article tickles your funny bone."

"I told you I didn't want your money. Yet, this agreement says I get a hundred thousand dollars on signing."

"The hundred grand is for a house."

"I have a house!"

"I know. But you said you have a mortgage. And I also realized that though you might make a lot of money in that job of yours in the future, as an employee at the bottom of the ladder you don't make all that much money now. So, the hundred thousand in the agreement is my share of making sure our baby has a home."

She considered the gesture for only a second before she said, "I don't want it."

"This baby is our responsibility—both of ours." He said the words gruffly, as if he didn't want her to make a big deal out of it. "I take my responsibilities seriously."

Tia stared at him for a second. Still dressed in his jeans and lightweight chambray shirt, he didn't look like a prosperous breeder. He looked more like one of the hands. But he *was* prosperous and this *was* his child and he *did* have a right to make sure his little boy or girl lived as well as he did. So, giving her that money wasn't a kind gesture. It wasn't even a fair thing to do. It was his way of assuring his child had a home.

She picked up the pen and signed the prenup.

"You ought to go over to your parents' tomorrow," Drew said, then took a big bite of his sandwich.

"I was there this afternoon. My mother and I covered everything we needed for the wedding. It's not going to be a big, splashy affair. More like a picnic with a few of us dressed formally. There's not really anything else for us to plan."

"Maybe not, but planning the wedding is one thing. Making sure your dad is blowing this off as no big deal is another. Did you talk to him today?"

"No, he stayed in the barn."

"That's why you need to drop by again tomorrow. He has to see you happy and casual about this whole deal so he will be, too."

Since that made sense, Tia nodded. "Okay. I'll go over tomorrow."

"After that, just drive back to Pittsburgh."

"Okay," she said, suddenly tired. Going from liking Drew to hating him to understanding him was draining. But no matter how coolly he treated her, she couldn't get away from the conclusion that he was a good man. A good person. She had to treat him fairly, but she had to find a way to do that without resurrecting her fairy tale that he was her Prince Charming. Because it was abundantly clear that he didn't want to be.

She ate her sandwich and had a glass of milk, then excused herself for bed. She woke the next morning still tired, so she rolled over and went back to sleep. When she finally did get out of bed, Drew was gone.

Adjusted to the fact that he planned to ignore her, she showered, dressed and drove to her parents' house. Though her mother chatted happily, filled with wedding ideas, her father barely said hello, and after he did, he raced off to the barn. He didn't appear upset with their situation but he hadn't talked to her in the two days since she'd announced she was marrying Drew.

She decided not to make too much of it, but pulling out of her parents' lane that afternoon, Tia unexpectedly thought about her brothers. This was how their separation from the family had started. Both did something their dad didn't like and in both situations their dad simply stopped talking. Ultimately, both Jericho and Rick had left town and now neither one of them even visited.

Still, she didn't think that would be her fate. After all, her dad didn't really seem angry. And she did know he was busy and preoccupied with the election. And the whole purpose of this charade was to downplay her pregnancy. Technically, his ignoring her proved that they had accomplished their purpose.

As she drove down the tree-lined country road on her way back to Pittsburgh, she approached the lane to Drew's horse farm. The natural instinct rose up in her to thank him for realizing the smart thing to do in their situation was to get married, but she knew she had to fight it. Drew might be a good man at heart, but he wouldn't want her thanks. He didn't really seem to want anything from her at all. Except that she stay out of his way.

By the time Tia returned to her house in Pittsburgh, she was exhausted from the drive and glad to be out of the town where she had to pretend to be joyfully in love with a man who hardly tolerated her.

Happy to be in familiar territory, she kicked off her shoes in her silent foyer and walked into her kitchen, where her answering machine was blinking.

She pressed the button and, more comfortable than she'd been in days, ambled to the refrigerator to pull out the orange juice.

"Tia!" the first message began. It was her boss. "If you're there, pick up!"

She grabbed a glass from the cupboard, confused by Glenn's harried tone.

"Pick up! Damn it!"

Hearing his voice shift from harried to angry, Tia froze in the center of her kitchen.

"Has anybody tried her cell phone?"

"I did." That voice was Lily Killian's. "My call went directly to voice mail. I'm guessing she doesn't have her cell turned on."

Tia squeezed her eyes shut. She'd turned off her cell, not wanting to be interrupted when she went to Drew's to tell him she was pregnant, and she'd forgotten to turn it back on.

"Damn it, Tia! When you get this message, call me. Barrington Cereal rejected our campaign. They called it a stupid piece of fluff. We're all working this weekend. Where are you?"

Chapter Three

When Tia opened her eyes on her wedding day, her stomach plummeted. She'd just been through the worst two weeks of her life and today she was marrying a man who didn't really want anything to do with her. When she'd called him to tell him that the work resulting from her firm's failed account didn't leave time for a honeymoon or even for her to come home that weekend, he'd been glad. *Glad.* Though she knew she shouldn't have been insulted, she couldn't help wondering how she'd get through eight months of weekends with a guy who had absolutely no intention of being nice to her. Not at all. Not ever.

The temptation to pull the covers over her head and forget about the whole damned world was strong, but she couldn't do it. She had a gown, a veil and a hundred pounds of chicken being barbecued by Ronnie Mc-Quillan. So what if she might soon be fired because it had been *her* idea that they'd used for the Barrington account? That was small potatoes compared to the fact that she was about to have a baby and she didn't want to reveal the circumstances of her pregnancy when her dad was already overwhelmed with stress from his first contested election in close to twenty years.

She did pull the covers over her head. Why was everything going wrong at the same time? She worked so hard to keep everything under control but suddenly she was being yelled at by her boss, marrying a man who didn't like her and trying to fool her father. Never in a million years would she have believed her life would turn out like this. But here she was in the middle of a mess.

Hearing a knock on her bedroom door, Tia slowly pulled the covers away from her face. "Who is it?"

Her mother entered carrying a tray. "Just me," she said happily. "I brought you breakfast." She set the tray on the bedside table as Tia sat up. "Even though the wedding's not till five you'll need the energy."

"Thanks."

Fussing over Tia's sleeveless white satin dress hanging from the back of the open closet door, Elizabeth said, "I don't want you to worry about a thing. Today is your special day."

This was another reason why Tia couldn't bail out on this wedding. Her mother had done absolutely everything she could to make this day perfect.

Summoning all her energy, Tia smiled and said,

"Thank you very much, Mom, for everything you've done. I'm sorry I couldn't help more."

Elizabeth smoothed her hand across the pink floral-print bedspread of Tia's bed. "Don't worry about it. I know from experience with your dad that work problems don't take a vacation just because you have something going on in your personal life." She grinned mischievously. "Besides, it was a lot of fun to plan your wedding. Especially without you. Now everything is exactly the way *I* always dreamed your wedding would be."

Tia laughed and her mother headed for the door. "There are a few last-minute details I need to attend to…"

"What can I do to help?"

"Nothing! I'm having a ball. Let me handle everything."

With that, Tia's mother left the room, and Tia fell back against the pillows of her bed. Her mother was too darned happy about a wedding that wasn't real. Her dad hadn't talked to her properly in the two weeks that had passed, even when she'd called to say hello. If he was as angry as she suspected he was, deciding to get married hadn't accomplished the purpose she and Drew wanted.

The whole situation was wrong. Wrong, wrong, wrong. Tia's brothers might be able to lie to their parents without qualms, but Tia could not do it. She had to fix this. Surely, now that her dad had had time to adjust to the fact that she was pregnant, she could explain that she didn't really want to marry Drew and get both herself and Drew out of a wedding neither of them wanted.

Actually, that sounded like a fine idea.

Quickly dressing in a pair of shorts and a T-shirt, Tia went in search of her father. After an hour of walking through barns and sheds, she found him in the foreman's office in the stable and gingerly knocked on the frame of the open door.

Her father glanced up from his discussion with the ruddy-faced foreman, Jim Tucker. "Tia? Why aren't you getting dressed?"

"Wedding doesn't start till five. It's not even noon yet."

"Don't you have some girlie thing to do?"

She laughed nervously. "Yes and no."

"Well, go do it."

She smiled shakily. "I'd like to talk to you, first."

Her father pulled in a breath and Tia watched Jim Tucker tense, reminding her of her father's condition. No matter how angry he was, if she called off the wedding she could actually make things worse.

Plus, there was that hundred pounds of chicken being barbecued. And she did already have a dress. And Drew was expecting to be able to give the baby his name. And the prenup was signed.

She took a step back. "You know what? I'm fine. I'll see you at five."

At three o'clock Tia's mother hustled Tia to her room. She filled her bathtub with warm water and bubbles, then left Tia with instructions to just relax.

An hour later she returned with Tia's two cousins—her bridesmaids in tow. Everybody seemed to be talking at once as Tia's little bedroom suddenly filled with huge garment bags containing full-skirted, rose-colored dresses and matching sun hats.

Maggie and Annie slipped into their gowns, and Tia's mother helped Tia into her tulle-skirted, satin bridal gown. When they were dressed, Elizabeth shepherded the bridesmaids out of the room before pulling a jewelry box from a drawer in Tia's dresser.

"What's this?"

Elizabeth smiled. "I hid it here this week so I could surprise you. It's a family tradition."

Tia drew a long breath, then opened the box that contained her grandmother's pearls. Her eyes round with confusion, she looked up at her mother. "You can't give me these! They were your mother's."

"And now they're yours. And when your daughter— if this is a daughter—" she said, patting Tia's still-flat tummy "—gets married, you can give them to her."

Overcome with guilt, Tia handed the box back to her mother. "No, Mom. I can't."

Elizabeth took the box, but not to put it back in the drawer. Instead, she lifted out the pearls and slid the strand around Tia's neck. "You have to." She hooked the clasp and let the translucent pearls fall to Tia's throat. "It's tradition."

With that, she walked to the door and opened it. "Let's go."

Tia fingered the pearls, but knowing she couldn't confess to her mother any more than she could call off the wedding, she decided the best course of action would be to take the pearls now and give them back after her divorce.

She took a breath. "The pearls are beautiful. Thanks."

"You're welcome," Tia's mother laughed. "For a second there I thought you were getting cold feet and you were about to say something like you couldn't go through with the wedding. Then I was going to panic! You may be able to deal with being pregnant and not married, but I'm still old-fashioned enough to want you married. Besides, Drew's a good man. I've always liked him. I couldn't ask for a better son-in-law. I'm glad you're marrying him."

She caught Tia's hand and pulled her into the corridor where Annie and Maggie waited at the top of the steps, and Tia had no choice but to allow herself to be swept down the stairs and to the den, where her father awaited her.

He didn't say a word. Though her mother fussed and the bridesmaids chattered, Ben stood stonily silent in front of the French doors, waiting for his cue to walk through with his daughter. Even after the pianist played the music that ushered Annie and Maggie up the aisle between the two rows of white folding chairs, he said nothing.

But as Tia and her father began the walk up the swath of crisp white paper that led to the little gazebo in front of her mother's garden of wildflowers, Tia forgot about her father. From the second she raised her gaze to look at the trio of men standing at the foot of the altar—the minister, the best man and her future husband—all she could think about was Drew.

He was drop-dead gorgeous in his tuxedo. The tailored garment showcased his height and the perfection of his build. But more than that, she suddenly realized that her mother was right. Drew *was* a good man. He'd come up with the plan to marry her to protect her dad. Without prompting or prodding he'd given his share of the price of her house to assure their baby had a home. Now he stood at the end of the aisle, smiling reassuringly at her, telling her with his expression that if she would trust him everything would be okay.

The pianist played a soft rendition of "Here Comes the Bride" and Tia's simple white gown rustled as she and her father walked up the aisle. The closer she got to the altar, the warmer Drew's smile became, and an odd feeling started to flutter in Tia's stomach. Drew's motives were nothing but good. And she did trust him. In some ways, the blind faith she'd put in Drew by agreeing to marry him was stronger than the faith of a typical bride.

Though she had to admit, she felt like a typical bride. Wearing her stunning dress and veil, with her mother's pearls, she felt beautiful. To the left, her teary-eyed mother gazed on, as if she couldn't believe her baby girl was all grown up.

To the right, Drew's groomsmen smiled their approval. In the center of the gazebo, the minister beamed. The scene was set for a real wedding, and if Tia's dad had been happier she'd probably have fallen victim to the whole darned fairy tale.

Her dad lifted her veil. "You look beautiful, princess," he said, then kissed her cheek.

His voice was so soft and so sincere that Tia's gaze flew to his. He smiled.

She whispered, "You're okay, now?"

"Yes," he whispered back. "Walking down the aisle, I realized that all this might be a big surprise to me, but you're an adult and you're obviously happy. So, I'm sorry I took my time about coming around." Before she could reply, he turned to give her to Drew.

Stunned, Tia took the hand Drew extended and absorbed the fact that her dad had just given her his blessing, capping the "real" feeling of her wedding. As if in the whole crazy world in which she now lived *this* was the one thing she was doing right.

Letting Drew grasp her hand, Tia took a breath and reminded herself that this wedding only felt "right" because some parts of this marriage really were right. Drew wanted to give their baby his name. He wanted to be officially involved in their baby's life. He didn't want her dad affected by their mistake. So, for all those reasons, her wedding was right.

On the other hand, the rest of her life was absolutely wrong. The first account idea she'd proposed to her team had fizzled. She'd lost the respect of her teammates. If she didn't prove soon to her boss that she wasn't a flake, she would be fired. So, of course, this wedding that her mother had planned, her father now sanctioned and her groom wanted seemed to be right.

She had to get her head out of the clouds or she would end up getting hurt.

But even after her perfect rationale, when the minister's opening remarks sounded like real instruction from her spiritual leader on how to be a good wife, Tia's feeling of rightness intensified. When she repeated her vows they weren't mere words. They sounded like promises. And she felt committed.

When Drew said his vows, she heard a vibration of sincerity in his deep, masculine voice and her breath shivered in her chest. She had to stop thinking of this wedding as real. It wasn't. Drew did not love her. If they were making a commitment, it was to their baby. Not to each other.

"You may kiss the bride."

Drew turned to Tia and their eyes met. His were dark and serious, clouded with something Tia now understood very well. Confusion. They had taken the biggest step a man and woman could take together. They had done it for some very good reasons. They'd even been smart enough to protect their finances with a prenup. But after her odd feelings during the ceremony, Tia realized there was so much more to this marriage than money. If their fifteen-minute service had almost sucked her into believing this was real, how would she possibly survive eight months?

I won't hurt you. I won't cheat you. You can trust me. She tried to say it with her eyes and a soft smile.

A few beats ticked off the clock before Drew seemed to understand what she was communicating to him. His own lips tilted upward slightly, as if he appreciated her reassurance, though he still believed it was hogwash.

Then he bent his head and touched his lips to hers, but before he could pull away, Tia slid her right arm around his neck and nudged him to stay where he was.

They wouldn't give the impression of two people so en-
amoured they'd had to get married within two weeks
with a peck on the lips. They had to genuinely kiss.

She felt the hesitation of his response, but he
deepened the kiss. The press of his mouth was so warm
and delicious that Tia relaxed her lips enough that they
parted. Smooth and delicious, his tongue slid over hers,
raising goose bumps on her flesh, sending invitation
coursing through her veins. She moved closer. His hands
went to her waist and pulled her closer still.

This was what she remembered of their night together. The passion. The pleasure. Except, this time
there was an added element. Emotion. It might not be
love. It might not even really be friendship. But they
were a team. If nothing else, they were partners.

Tia felt herself slipping, remembering their night
together, wondering if this really was a mistake—or if
it was fate. Drew had been everything she'd wanted for
so many years, it seemed impossible to believe this
wasn't exactly what was supposed to be happening.

A low chuckle erupted from the crowd and Tia very
distinctly heard her dad clear his throat. Beside them the
minister shifted uncomfortably.

Drew pulled away, but kept his eyes locked on hers.
Tia swallowed hard. The sexual chemistry between
them was powerful. He had more good traits than bad.
They had conceived a child. The thought that fate or
destiny had brought them here poured through her
again, almost making her dizzy with wanting.

But, as always, Drew made a joke. "Sorry about that,"

he said to the crowd in general. "But you know how newlyweds are. Next time somebody just toss a bucket of water on us."

Tia felt her face redden as the crowd roared with laughter. She was about to forget every good thought she'd had about him and dub him completely hopeless, but behind the flare of the tulle skirt of her gown, he caught her hand and squeezed gently.

Confusion nearly overwhelmed her. Even as he made light of their relationship, he seemed to find a way to back-handedly tell her everything was okay between them.

They walked down the aisle, followed by brides-maids and groomsmen who formed a line to greet guests. Mostly they were neighbors, and Tia happily accepted their congratulations, cautioning herself not to get pulled in. It would be so easy to get caught up in the fairy tale. Particularly if Drew kept showing her his good side. She had to remember that this marriage was temporary. Even their prenup spelled out the terms of their divorce.

Tia said a final goodbye to the minister and turned to the next guest in the receiving line, but before she knew what was happening she was enveloped in a huge bear hug by a man she didn't know and a smacking kiss landed on her cheek. Then she was pushed back so the man could inspect her as if she were a thoroughbred about to go on the block for sale.

"Damned if you aren't right again, Drew. She is about the prettiest thing this side of New York City."

"Friend of the groom?" Tia guessed with a laugh,

hoping her lungs would reinflate sometime soon after the strength of that hug.

"Friend of the groom?" the petite woman at the bear-man's side mumbled unhappily. "Drew! Haven't you told her about us?"

Her curiosity piqued, because Drew had invited out-of-town friends, Tia extended her hand to the woman. "I'm Tia."

"I'm Drew's mother," the pretty little redhead said, and Tia knew her mouth fell open in surprise.

"Drew's mother!"

"Before Drew's ex-wife got ahold of him," Drew's mother said, "he actually had manners and he probably would have introduced us himself. Since his former wife turned him into Attila the Hun, he doesn't have the manners of a polar bear. So I'll introduce myself. I'm Vivian."

"It's nice to meet you, Vivian," Tia managed, reeling with confusion. She knew Drew would have told his parents he was about to be a dad. She knew he might even have explained the marriage of convenience, but because they were from Oklahoma, she never in a million years had thought he would invite them to a fake wedding.

"This is my husband, Tom."

"Big Tom!" Drew's dad corrected before he drew Tia into another bone-crushing hug.

"Big Tom," she agreed, her voice small and breath-less because he was cutting off her air.

"Let's not forget she's pregnant, Dad," Drew whispered, low enough for his dad to hear but not so loud as to be overheard by anyone near them. "You don't want to be manhandling her until after the baby's born."

Big Tom let her go. "Right. Sorry."

"That's okay," Tia choked out, subtly trying to gasp for breath as she realized Drew might have told his parents about the baby, but she didn't think he'd explained this was a fake marriage. "I'm so glad you're here."

"I wish Drew had told you we were coming."

"Mom, there's a shrimp cocktail over there with your name on it."

Vivian Wallace laughed gaily. "You want a few minutes to get yourself out of this."

"I *need* a few minutes to get myself out of this."

Big Tom seemed to understand completely. "Let's go get some of that shrimp, Vivvi."

The second they were out of earshot, another couple stepped forward in the receiving line. Drew and Tia accepted their congratulations and the congratulations of about twenty more friends and neighbors before the line dwindled and Drew's best man, Matt Melbourne, the local vet, handed them both a cool glass of water.

"Drink this before we head over to the main table for dinner and a toast. It will replenish your fluids."

"It *is* hot."

"But beautiful," Tia said, glancing around. Above the green hills of Virginia, the sky was solid blue, perfect. With the wedding handled and her father happy again, Tia could almost believe this part of her life was going to be okay—due in no small part to Drew, who took his commitment so seriously he hadn't even confided the truth about the wedding to his parents.

"Matt, could you give Tia and me a minute alone?"

"You're probably going to have to go into the house to get a minute alone."

"Right," Drew said and took her hand. He easily guided her through the crowd, accepting more congratulations and answering comments, but not stopping until they were behind the closed door of her dad's den.

"I should have introduced you to my parents."

"Yes, that would have been nice," she agreed, but ever since their time at the altar everything had changed between them. They really were partners, and partners didn't argue or undermine. They worked together. "But we're in a very unusual situation. And I haven't been home for two weeks. I can see how it fell through the cracks." Then, before he could reply, she added, "I like them."

"They're as weird as I am."

"No," she disagreed, shaking her head slightly and smiling at him. "They seem like very comfortable people. I think they're going to make really great grandparents."

"Good. Because something else I forgot to tell you is that I'm an only child. This baby will be their only grandchild. They're gonna spoil it silly."

"Okay. That's all good to know."

He waited a few heartbeats as if expecting something else, then he said, "You're sure you're not mad?"

She smiled. "Positive."

"You don't want to give me some kind of sermon about keeping secrets?"

She shook her head. "No. As I said, the situation is odd, Drew. We both have to roll with some punches."

"Okay," he agreed cautiously, then walked to the door and held it open for her. "Let's go get some supper."

"Sounds great. I'm starving." She paused at the doorway and peeked over her shoulder at him. "You have no idea of the appetite of a pregnant woman. Hang on to your chicken, Drew, because once I start eating I can't be held responsible."

He laughed and caught Tia's hand and Tia felt an odd kind of power surge through her. She'd done it. By accepting the situation and not stressing out over things that couldn't be changed, she'd avoided an argument. And he was happy with her. And things were going to run smoothly.

She would need to remember this on Monday morning when she returned to work and was confronted by six people who absolutely hated her because her lousy idea had created double work for them.

"When Drew told me he was getting married again," Matt said, his champagne glass raised in a toast, "I nearly had a heart attack. I said, 'Buddy, didn't you learn anything from the first woman who ripped your heart out, stomped it to smithereens and then took all your money?'"

The crowd broke into uproarious laughter and Matt grinned happily, but Tia's head tilted. That was the second mention she'd heard of Drew's other relationship, and though an hour ago she might not have cared, with her desire to keep at least one area of her life working, she knew this was significant.

"But when he told me he was marrying Tia, I stopped dead in my tracks. First, considering Drew's reputation, I couldn't believe Ben let him get within fifty yards of his daughter."

Again the crowd laughed.

"Second, I couldn't believe Tia would have anything to do with him."

The crowd laughed again, but Tia only smiled. Though it was true this was a marriage of convenience, and also true that Drew was a little rough around the edges, she knew damned well any unmarried woman in the room over the age of sixteen would get involved with him in a heartbeat.

"But I'm glad she did," Matt continued, raising his glass in a toast. "Here's to the happy couple."

Not quite sure what to expect, Tia peered cautiously at her new husband. To her great relief, he was genuinely smiling. He tipped his glass to her, urging her to entwine her arms with his so the photographer could get a nice picture of their official wedding toast. Tia smiled and did as he asked. They really seemed to be getting the hang of being partners.

When dinner was over, Tia and Drew walked hand-in-hand, mingling with their guests. Drew got involved in a particularly intense conversation and before Tia knew what had happened, they were separated. Just as quickly, his mother was at her side.

"Hello."

She took a quick breath and smiled warmly. "Hello, Vivian."

"You're not at all what I expected Drew's next wife would be like."

Tia laughed. "Maybe that's a good thing?"

Vivian linked her arm through Tia's and began walking toward a shady tree, away from the crowd. "Maybe it is."

"You're about to have some kind of mother-of-the-groom talk with me, aren't you?" Tia teased, since Vivian and Tom seemed to have the same off-beat personalities as their son.

"Yes, but maybe not the kind you expect," Vivian admitted with a wince. "I know my son," she said when they were out of hearing distance of most of the crowd. "He's angry, and he's bitter."

"He's also very fair, honorable and kind," Tia said, listing the positive traits she'd discovered about Drew.

Vivian laughed. "So you see the good?"

"It's hard to miss," Tia said, smiling at Drew's mom. She seemed to be a kindhearted woman who only wanted what was best for her child. About to be a mother herself, Tia understood that perfectly.

"I still think I need to tell you a few things."

"No. Really, everything's fine," Tia insisted, not wanting to get drawn into a conversation that could come back to haunt them—or, more accurately, hurt Vivian. Tia didn't want to give Vivian a wrong impression that would leave her disappointed when Tia and Drew divorced.

"Everything might look fine," Vivian said, patting Tia's arm, which she still held. "But I'll feel better if you understand a few things. Drew's first wife was awful." Vivian grimaced. "But Drew never saw it. She didn't even have to take him to court to get a fair settlement. Without argument or prodding, he'd given her half of everything they owned. Even the firm he'd helped start before they were married. Then Drew discovered she was having an affair with his business partner. That was the hard part. He'd been fair and kind to a woman who had betrayed him and he really felt she'd taken him for a ride." Vivian sighed and shrugged. "I think you get the picture."

"Yes." Tia nodded. "He had a really bad first marriage."

"And he's bitter and he's angry and I don't think you've known each other long enough for you to have helped him through that."

Deciding not to lie, particularly since this was a perfect avenue to pave the way for their upcoming divorce, Tia said, "You might be right."

"So I want you to promise to be patient."

Tia swallowed. How could she promise to be patient when she and Drew already knew they'd divorce? Grasping for something to say, all Tia could think of was, "I'm really going to try."

"Because the thing nobody knows about Drew is that he took the loss of that marriage really, really hard. He pretends he was angry about the money and the affair. But the truth is, losing the woman he genuinely loved hurt him. So that's why he is the way he is, but I think that if you'll just give him time, you'll bring him around."

Tia smiled slowly, her heart breaking, not for her or even for Drew, but for his mother. But, at least they were giving Vivian a grandchild. And at least Tia now understood why Drew was so suspicious. "I understand."

"Good," Vivian said, then walked Tia back to the party.

Drew was about to go looking for Tia when her father approached him.

"Drew, if you don't mind," Ben began, but he shook his head and then chuckled. "Actually, even if you do mind, you and I need to have a word in the den."

Drew inclined his head. He'd known this was coming. The only thing that surprised him was that Ben had waited so long. He'd expected Ben to come to his house a week ago and rake him over hot coals, at the very least for not mentioning his relationship with Ben's daughter, so the discussion was long overdue. He was about to get the sermon of his life and he intended simply to take it like a man.

When they stepped into Ben's office and Ben closed the door behind him, he said only, "I'm sorry."

"Sorry?" Drew parroted stupidly.

Ben drew a quick breath. "Look, I'm not a simpleton. I understand that age doesn't always factor into romance. I know my daughter is beautiful. She's also smart and funny and will make a wonderful wife. I should have realized that some day you would wake up and see that."

Dumbstruck, Drew wasn't entirely sure what to say. If he was hearing correctly, he was off the hook.

"And I know she's always had a crush on you."

Drew turned from the fireplace. This was new information. "Really?"

Ben laughed. "Oh, come on, you had to have seen it. Her mother and I used to chuckle about how she'd trip over her own feet when you were around."

"I thought she was clumsy."

"Oh, Drew," Ben said, laughing again. "Do yourself a favor and don't ever tell her that!"

"I won't," Drew said, but he felt strange. Not only had he been absolved of his sin, but now he also knew that Tia, the woman who seemed to like to spit fire at him, had always had a crush on him. It should have given him a chuckle. Instead, it twisted something in the vicinity of his heart. He'd never given her the time of day. He'd called her foolish things like Squirt. It also explained why they had made love the night they'd met in Pittsburgh.

"Let's get back out to the party," Ben said, nodding toward the door.

Drew took a breath and followed Ben's lead. But when he reached the door, Ben slapped him on the back.

"Just remember, if you ever hurt her, I will have to hunt you down and shoot you."

Because it was the sort of joke they'd shared before Drew got Ben's daughter pregnant, Drew laughed. "Got it," he said, then led Ben back to the patio and the reception festivities.

He and Ben were separated almost the moment they stepped out amongst the pots of daisies and vases of fragrant roses on the patio. Drew immediately spotted Tia and began walking toward her.

He caught her hand just as the lead singer for the band her mother had hired approached them.

"We're set up now," the singer said, looking from Tia to Drew and then back at Tia again. He appeared to be twenty-eight or so. His hair was short and spiky. The dull gray shirt and tattered jeans he wore screamed of an antiestablishment, free-spirited entertainer personality. He also had warm blue eyes that continually strayed to Tia's face. "So we're ready anytime you are. First dance is yours."

Drew almost said, "Might as well get this over with," but he remembered what Ben had said about Tia having a crush on him most of her teen years. He swallowed, then said, "Sure, we're ready, too. What do you want us to do?"

"Stand on the edge of the patio that Ben has marked off for dancing. We'll introduce you. You dance."

Tia smiled. "Sounds simple enough."

"Hey," the singer said, his voice light, lilting, flirtatious. "I've been doing this for ten years. I promise I'll make it completely painless."

Tia laughed, enjoying him, and something foreign rippled through Drew. She might have had a crush on Drew in her teen years, it might have even been the remnants of that crush that made her invite him home in Pittsburgh, but she was an adult now. Pretty, intelligent, interesting to men her own age. And Drew had been nothing but a grouchy pain in the butt who insisted she marry him, insisted he get a place in their baby's life, insisted she sign a prenup, without once saying a kind word or even thanks. He knew the child he had with her would be his only child. Yet, he hadn't been smart enough to appreciate Tia.

The singer bounded off, taking his spot behind the microphone as Tia and Drew made their way to the makeshift dance floor. The band began to play something slow and the lead singer introduced Drew and Tia, who glided out to dance.

Drew slid his hand around her waist and she put her free hand on his shoulder and they circled the dance floor. He hadn't intended to make a big deal out of their marriage, or this wedding, but now everything was off-kilter. He blamed her dad for telling him she had had a crush on him, then he blamed the lead singer for reminding him that Tia was a beautiful woman, but he knew that the real culprit was his libido…or maybe his pride.

This beautiful woman was now officially his. And she was carrying his child. And he didn't want other men looking at her and he did want to sleep with her.

He had a feeling somebody was going to have to come up with an awfully compelling argument to convince him to keep his hands off her tonight when they got home.

Chapter Four

Tia sneaked a peek at Drew as he slid behind the wheel of his Mercedes to drive them home from their reception.

He'd been acting strangely since their first dance: one minute quiet, the next solicitous. And Tia herself had been feeling funny since his mother had made her promise to take care of him. She didn't know the reason for Drew's odd behavior, but she knew why she felt differently. His mother had told her enough about Drew's past that Tia now understood why he always said something that made her mad when it seemed they might be getting too friendly. He'd been hurt. He'd been cheated, lied to, stolen from. He didn't want to be hurt again. In short, he didn't want another marriage.

Which was great, because knowing his feelings about

marriage helped her to not fall victim to the powerful emotions she'd felt when he'd held her on the dance floor and when she'd thrown her bouquet. It even helped her to ignore the nervous excitement trembling through her at the knowledge that they were about to enter his house as man and wife.

Drew pulled his car up to the front porch of his house, cut the engine and got out. Tia reached for her door handle but before she opened the door, he was already there to help her exit. She smiled.

"Thanks."

"You're welcome." His voice was soft and serious, so intense it was beginning to scare her. Not because she was afraid of him. She was afraid of what would happen to her if she got involved with him for real. Knowing that he had a failed relationship might help her to see why he was resistant to embarking on another, but understanding didn't mean she was so foolish as to think she would be the woman who would change his mind. Once the baby was born, he intended to divorce her. *That* was what she had to remember.

She allowed him to help her and her full-skirted gown out of his car, but let go of his hand the minute she was on her feet. Without waiting for him, she turned to the porch stairs and, hiking her skirt to her calves for ease of mobility, she ran up the three steps.

Again, when she reached the door, he was there before she was and opened it for her.

She smiled her thanks and turned to walk in, but he grabbed her arm.

His dark eyes caught her gaze. "Aren't you forgetting something?"

The hungry look in his eyes rendered her speechless and she couldn't think, let alone figure out what it was he thought she was forgetting. Before she got a chance to reason it out, he scooped her up into his arms. Thrust against his chest and held in his strong arms only a few inches away from his face, she froze.

In her dreams, she'd pictured scenarios like this over and over, but nothing came close to the reality. The ease with which he lifted her demonstrated his strength and made him seem like the kind of man a woman could depend on. When she flung her arms around his neck to steady herself, his soft hair tickled her fingers. His heady male scent found her nostrils.

This was not good. Especially since she knew how well muscled he was beneath the tux and crisp white shirt. She knew he had a mat of dark chest hair. She knew his texture and his taste. She knew making love with him was glorious.

Her pulse quickened, but she reminded herself he didn't want her. Not really. Not forever. And if he didn't want her forever and she slept with him, she would get hurt. Despite her rationale, it took every ounce of restraint she had not to nestle against him. Not to nuzzle her nose against the firm skin of his neck. Not to tickle or tease, whisper romantic phrases, give in to the sexual attraction that pulsed between them.

He strode through the open door, talking. "As you heard at the wedding, I haven't had much luck at marriage. It dawned on me that might have been because I wasn't much for tradition or conventionality, so this time around I'm not taking any chances."

Tia swallowed. *He wasn't taking any chances?* What was that supposed to mean? They'd already agreed that this marriage would end when the baby was born. And she'd lectured herself about getting involved in anything that might ultimately hurt her...or him. Technically, she'd promised his mother she wouldn't hurt him.

"Does it matter if we break with a tradition or two since we're getting divorced?"

He captured her gaze again with his intense brown eyes and Tia held her breath. If his expression was anything to go by, he was having second thoughts about making this marriage real—at least physically. Every fiber of her being longed to give him anything and everything he wanted. Every cell in her brain, however, reminded her that confusing their deal by making love would only make the divorce painful.

Finally Drew said, "We have almost eight months to be married. Even considering that we'll only see each other a few weekends, we will be spending those entire weekends together and that's a lot of time. Plenty of things can go wrong in eight months of weekends. That's why I don't want to take any chances."

Though disappointment rumbled through Tia, her common sense breathed a sigh of relief.

"Yeah. Best not to take any chances."

Still, he didn't put her down, and when too much time passed with him holding her, she quickly recalled every word he'd just said, wondering if she'd missed something. When she got to the part about lots of things going wrong, she realized exactly the opposite was true, too. A lot of things could also go right.

She caught his gaze, understanding his hesitation. If enough things went right, these eight months could be a stepping stone to falling in love for real. And if they fell in love for real, then they wouldn't divorce…and nobody would get hurt. And if nobody was going to get hurt, was it so wrong to make love?

She licked her dry lips. That was wishful thinking at its finest. And why shouldn't she be thinking wishfully? Every other area of her life sucked. Her original cereal campaign ideas weren't as good as they should have been. The rest of the ad team seemed to be losing faith in her. It was no wonder staying in Virginia and being married to a sex god seemed like heaven. It was the easy way out.

She took a breath, reminding herself that she loved her career and she wasn't a coward. So what if her first real idea failed? She had to fight her way out of this and prove herself. And she couldn't very well do that from a farm a six-hour drive away from her office. No matter how sexy Drew was, or how real their vows had seemed, he wasn't really hers. And if she got caught up in this charade, thinking he loved her when he was only playing house, biding his time until the baby was born and he could divorce her, she would be so devastated there was a good possibility that she'd lose her career.

"You might want to put me down."

He looked ready to argue, but Tia said, "I mean it."

He gazed into her eyes for a few seconds longer but Tia held her ground. Their agreement was set. They'd actually spelled it out on paper in the prenup and both had signed on the dotted line. She'd be a fool if she believed the look of longing in his eyes over his signature. Drew was too much of a pragmatist. His signature always trumped his feelings.

"Come on, Drew. Just like you said, it's best not to take any unnecessary chances."

He slid her to the floor. "Right."

"I think I'll go to bed now," Tia said brightly, immediately easing them out of the awkwardness of standing around and chatting, or trying to figure out something to do for the next hour or so. "I left my overnight case with extra clothes and toiletries in the bedroom I was using the weekend I stayed here…you know…when we decided to get married. So I'll just go back to that room."

He glanced in the living room, at the bar, and Tia didn't blame him. A good, stiff drink sounded like a great idea to her, too. If she could have had one, she would.

He returned his gaze to hers, his eyes uncertain, wavering. He might have put her down, but he hadn't really decided against making love. Tia didn't move, didn't breathe. It was one thing for her to decide on her own that making love wasn't a good idea, but it would be another thing entirely to be strong if he kissed her, touched her, began to seduce her. She knew the power of his kisses and she wasn't sure she was strong enough to resist.

Regret filled his eyes, then he smiled wearily and said, "Good night."

Not about to press her luck, Tia fled up the steps, breathing a sigh of relief that her questionable resolve hadn't been put to the test.

In the yellow bedroom she'd used on her first weekend stay, she kicked off her satin slippers, tossed her veil to the dresser and unhooked the strand of pearls that had belonged to her grandmother. She wasn't wearing panty hose or a bra. The dress didn't leave her the option of a bra and it was July. Panty hose would have been torture. So she only had to remove her dress and a pair of panties before she could get into the shower and slide into comfortable pajamas and between crisp, cool sheets.

She twisted to grip the back zipper of the dress and it slid down easily, but when she tried to yank it off, it wouldn't budge. Confused, she reached behind her again and discovered that the top was held together by a hook and eye. She shifted her hands, grasped the hook and attempted to maneuver it, but she couldn't get it to release.

Drat!

Barefoot, she padded back down the stairs, once again holding her gown to her calves, probably looking like Cinderella running out of the prince's ball at the stroke of midnight.

Drew stood in the living room by the bay window, staring out at the starry night, holding a drink in a crystal glass.

At the door, she cleared her throat so she didn't scare him when she spoke. He spun away from the window and their gazes caught and held.

Before he could draw any incorrect conclusions, she said, "Sorry, but I can't get my dress unhooked."

He set his drink on the bar as she made her way into the living room. "You need help?"

"Yeah. Sorry." Nervous, she added, "There's a hook and eye back there."

He slid his fingers under the top of the back of her strapless dress and glided them underneath the fabric, tickling her skin as he searched for the closure.

"Just find that and unhook it and I'll be on my way."

His voice was thick and smoky when he said, "Okay."

The pads of his fingers skimmed her back, raising gooseflesh as he took a second pass beneath the neckline of her dress. "I can't seem to find it."

"It's small." Her voice shivered from her as the feeling of his fingers against her skin resurrected memories of their night together. "Damn it. Hurry."

The zipper of the dress was already down, so when the hook and eye released the bodice of the gown instantly sagged. She caught in the last second before anything private was exposed, but air brushed her now-naked back and her whole body began to tingle.

She pasted on a smile and turned to face him, crushing her slack gown to her chest. "Thanks."

Drew swallowed and softly said, "You're welcome."

Tia nodded and scampered out of the room.

"Good morning."

Drew sucked in a breath to control the surge of hormones that erupted just at the sound of her voice.

He'd been so damned tempted to sleep with her the night before that he had forgotten about his ex-wife. Luckily, Tia herself had saved him. From the starstruck look in her eyes it was clear that if they made love, she would believe their marriage was real.

That had hit him like a ton of bricks, because he knew a few things she might not know about real marriages. They ended. That in and of itself wasn't so bad, except that when any partnership ended, people got hurt. He might have taken care of the financial end of things with the prenup, but there was nothing anybody could do about the emotional backlash. Tia would hate him. He'd hate her. That was just the way it went. Though he knew that he could probably get over another heartbreak, and Tia would, too, the wildcard in this situation was her dad—his friend. If things ended badly, Ben would have to pick a side. And Drew didn't think he'd side with him. If he and Tia stuck to their original agreement, and didn't get any stupid ideas about making this a real marriage, they would divorce civilly. Nobody would hate anybody. Everybody would be relieved. And Ben wouldn't have to pick sides.

"If you had slept another twenty minutes, Mrs. Hernandez would have sent you out to the barn to eat hay for breakfast."

"Oh, I would have done no such thing!" Drew's housekeeper said, scurrying to the table so she could slap the back of his head. A short, stout woman of Mexican descent, Mrs. Hernandez wasn't afraid of Drew and Drew knew she was always good for a little comic relief to take the edge off awkward situations.

"Good morning, Tia," she said, pulling out Tia's chair. "I can't believe this. I go away for a few weeks to take care of my sister and when I get back you're married. God only knows why any sane woman would want this man, but I'm glad somebody finally does."

"Tia's not sane."

"I am so sane," she countered as she waved away the housekeeper's offer of coffee. "And Mrs. Hernandez knows that because she plays cards with my mother."

Mrs. Hernandez brandished the coffeepot at Drew. "And that means if you don't treat this girl well, I can tell her mother."

"I'm not afraid of Elizabeth," Drew said, but even as he said the words he wondered if he shouldn't be. The night he and Tia had announced their impending marriage to Ben and Elizabeth, Elizabeth had been quickly drawing the correct conclusion that something wasn't quite right. Drew had barely gotten himself and Tia out of her house without an inquisition, but after that, Elizabeth's suspicions had seemed to disappear as she'd happily planned the wedding, and Drew had forgotten all about them.

But if Mrs. Hernandez said the wrong thing at her card club, Elizabeth's misgivings might return and she might start asking questions they didn't want to answer.

Still, he couldn't let his housekeeper see she had the upper hand. Instead, he smiled at her. "Besides, nobody believes anything you say."

"Why do I work here?" Mrs. Hernandez mumbled as she walked away from the table.

"The pay is good," Drew called after her. When she was out of earshot, he turned to Tia. "If she knows your mother, we might have a problem."

"They play cards together." Tia toyed with the silverware by her place mat.

"Which means they gossip."

"Talk."

"Whatever."

Tia drew a breath that pulled Drew's attention to the way her breasts strained the soft material of her tank-style pajama top. His desperate need from the night before flooded back, but he ignored it, motivated more by keeping his deal with Tia than his libido.

"We have to be careful how we behave so that she doesn't catch on to the fact that we hardly know each other."

"That only means we have to pretend to like each other when she's around."

Drew shook his head. "You're not understanding what I'm telling you. She *lives* here."

"And I'll only be here on weekends," Tia reminded him, not meeting his eyes, again overly interested in her silverware.

Drew frowned. There wasn't a darned thing wrong with her fork and spoon, yet she kept moving them as if it mattered which one sat where. Not wanting to make too big of a deal out of it for fear Mrs. Hernandez would notice her nervousness, Drew returned his attention to the newspaper and casually asked, "Are you okay this morning?"

"Sure. I'm great."

"You seem to be mighty interested in the order of your fork and spoon." He heard his housekeeper approach the table and quickly changed the subject. "Tell Mrs. Hernandez what you want for breakfast."

"Eggs," she said, smiling at the eager woman waiting to serve her. "And toast."

"Piece of cake," Mrs. Hernandez said and began to walk away.

But Tia said, "Cake. You know, some pancakes would taste really good, too."

Mrs. Hernandez turned and smiled. "Eggs. Toast. Pancakes. Sounds good."

She took another two steps before Tia said, "Do you have any hash browns?"

Mrs. Hernandez stopped. "No, but I can make them."

"Good," Tia said, rising from her seat. "Maybe I'll just grab a piece of fruit while I wait."

Mrs. Hernandez gaped at her. "How in the name of all that is holy do you stay so thin?"

"We're not telling anybody yet," Drew said, concluding that the best way to keep Mrs. Hernandez from looking too closely at their relationship was to distract her, "but Tia's pregnant. Just feed her."

Mrs. Hernandez stopped dead in her tracks. "Pregnant!" she crooned. "We're going to have a baby!"

"Tia and I are going to have a baby. You're going to have more laundry."

"I love laundry!" she said, and scurried away, surreptitiously wiping her eyes.

"That was pretty crafty."

"I know how to handle her," Drew said, glancing around his kitchen at the dark oak cupboards with the shiny, slate-gray granite countertops. The room was simple, but he made sure that Mrs. Hernandez had every convenience and small appliance available at her disposal. He might give her a rough time, but she had it pretty good here so she wouldn't quit. The only problem was that she might inadvertently reveal personal things to Elizabeth that could give them away.

"I still think we've got a problem."

Tia shook her head in dismay. "I'm beginning to see you're a worrier."

"I'm more of a planner. If we really were in love and married," he said, glancing over to make sure Mrs. Hernandez was out of earshot, "we wouldn't be out of bed yet. We wouldn't have gotten up separately. And that guest room wouldn't have been slept in."

"Oh, shoot," Tia said through a groan. "You're right."

"I'll slip out in a minute and go upstairs and make the bed in the guest room. Then as soon as you can, you get your stuff into my room."

He caught her gaze and she said nothing. But she didn't have to. They'd just barely managed to avoid making love the night before and tonight they would be sleeping in the same room. They wouldn't have the escape of sleeping apart. They would be side by side in his king-size bed.

The sexual tension that had hummed between them the night before filled the room again. He saw the need in her blue eyes as clearly as he felt his own desire tighten his body.

Still, he was the older, wiser partner in this deal and, if it killed him, he would be strong. "Don't worry. Like you said, it's only for weekends and I can sleep on the floor."

"You shouldn't have to sleep on the floor."

"You have a better idea?" he asked, then loudly added, "Plus, Mrs. Hernandez can babysit."

"I heard that," the housekeeper said as she scurried over to serve Tia a plate of eggs and toast. "Pancakes are on their way."

"I know you heard," Drew said. "That's just my way of letting you know *I* can hear *you* when you try to sneak up on me."

"Smart aleck."

Mrs. Hernandez walked away and Drew leaned close to Tia. "She's crazy about me."

"She thinks you're insane, the same as I do."

"Then my work here is done." He rose from the table. "Get your things out of the guest room as soon as you're done eating," he whispered as he leaned in to kiss her. She stared at him with her big blue eyes and everything inside Drew leapt to life, all but begging him to change his mind about making love. But that was out of the question because that would change the dynamic of their divorce, and a nasty divorce wasn't acceptable.

He pressed his lips to hers and kissed her long enough that Mrs. Hernandez wouldn't wonder, but also long enough to get all of his adrenaline pumping and his hormones doing a happy dance.

He swore he heard those same hormones groan when he pulled away, but just as he'd already reminded himself, this was the right thing to do.

Chapter Five

Tia left the breakfast table and nonchalantly slipped upstairs to clear her things out of the guest room and get herself settled in the master suite. Repacking the suitcase wasn't difficult. All she had to do was zip it closed and toss it onto the bed, which Drew had made as he'd promised. Her gown and veil were on a hanger in a garment bag with her shoes. All in all, it took her two minutes to get everything ready to move.

With her cosmetic bag under one arm, her garment bag over her shoulder and her suitcase in her hand, she peeked out the bedroom door. No one. She didn't even hear Mrs. Hernandez humming. She was totally alone.

Still, she didn't waste a second getting to the room at the end of the hall. She rushed down the corridor, pushed open the door with her shoulder, dumped her things on the floor and then closed the door behind her.

Her heart thumped with the fear of getting caught, but as she glanced around Drew's bedroom, it picked up even more. His suite was fantastic.

A black-and-white, geometric-design bedspread lay across the king-size bed. Black-and-white pillows of all shapes, sizes and designs littered the space beneath the headboard. Shiny black bedside tables held pewter lamps and red candles. Matching wing chairs sitting on a red area rug created a sophisticated conversation area in the curve of the bay window, which, with the curtains pulled back, provided a panoramic view of the green hills of Drew's farm.

The walls held black-and-white photographs of horses prancing to the winner's circle or in the winner's circle. Tia guessed they were horses Drew had bred. The room was chic, but masculine, and reminded her that there was so much about Drew that she didn't know. It also reminded her that he was more experienced than she was, more worldly. Two weeks ago she might have said that didn't matter, but having endured her failure at work, she suddenly saw that it did.

She walked to the bed and ran her fingers across the smooth silk comforter, trying to talk herself out of being nervous by reminding herself that Drew was an architect. And as for how well-appointed his house was, she'd long ago suspected he'd hired a decorator. Sure, he was older than she was. Yes, he had knowledge and experience that she didn't. But she wasn't a child. She also wasn't an idiot. She was pretty smart herself. And as for experience, she was getting it in spades just by dealing with him.

Besides, she only had to interact with him on weekends. If she had to be with him twenty-four hours a day, seven days a week, she might have opportunities to make a fool of herself. As it was, she would only see him forty-eight hours a week. She would be fine.

By the time she had her few shirts, capris, jeans and undergarments in the drawers of the empty dresser she found in the huge walk-in closet, and her gown hanging in the back, she felt like her normal, confident self. But when she walked out onto the front porch with her laptop, intending to do some work while Drew was in the barn, she saw Rayne Fegan pulling into Drew's driveway, and her confidence took a direct hit.

She didn't know what kind of bug had bitten Rayne that she felt she had to get Tia's dad out of office. That was yet another reality Tia had to deal with.

"Hi, Tia," Rayne called as she stepped out of her little blue car. About five-six with naturally blond hair that she always wore in a ponytail or wrapped in a bun, Rayne was a pretty girl who downplayed her appearance in favor of promoting her intelligence. If the lack of makeup and ponytail didn't get that point across, then the neutral-colored T-shirts she wore with too-big jeans usually did.

"How are you this morning?"

"I'm fine, Rayne," Tia said, annoyance seeping into her voice though she tried hard to stop it.

"That's good." Rayne walked to the front porch. "Sorry about visiting the day after your wedding, but the minister accidentally stuffed your marriage certificate into his jacket pocket yesterday. After services this morning he asked me to deliver it."

Tia looked at the envelope Rayne was handing to her, then lifted her gaze to meet Rayne's. Rayne smiled and Tia didn't see the face of an enemy or even a stranger. Today, Rayne simply looked like Tia's old friend. The other outcast. The person in whom Tia had confided. The one who knew how long Tia had had a crush on Drew Wallace. And maybe the only person who wouldn't be at all surprised that Tia had married him.

"Thanks."

Rayne smiled sheepishly. "He told me your wedding was very nice."

"It was," Tia said, suddenly awash with guilt that she hadn't invited the one person who really had been her friend in high school. "I'm sorry I didn't invite you," she said awkwardly. "But you know, you and I kind of drifted apart in the past few years."

To her surprise, Rayne laughed. "And I *am* throwing slings and arrows at your dad."

"But why?" Tia asked, abundantly confused. The Rayne Fegan Tia remembered was a smart girl who only wanted to be taken seriously. Sure, she'd had a schoolgirl crush on Tia's older brother Jericho, but though that had embarrassed her, it wasn't enough to turn Rayne into an enemy. More than that, Rayne wasn't the kind of person to gossip or even get involved in small-town politics. She had always been certain she was destined for bigger and better things. Yet here she was in the little town she hated, doing the very things she swore she'd never do.

"My dad hasn't ever done anything to you—"

"He's never done anything at all, Tia."

Tia gasped.

Rayne sighed. "Oh, come on. There's been no increase in services since he took over. He's brought in no jobs for the hundreds of young people who have been forced to move closer to D.C. to find work." She sighed again. "Face it, Tia, he's a good old boy. He intends to keep things the way they've always been so he and his friends continue to prosper." She paused and shook her head. "Look who I'm talking to. You married one of those good old boys who wants everything to stay the same." She took a deep breath and turned to go. "See you around."

With that, she jogged down the steps and Tia stared after her. She understood what Rayne was saying, but she also understood her father's perspective. Progress wasn't always good. Bigger wasn't always better. Calhoun Corners was a town created by the needs of the surrounding horse farmers. As far as the families who still owned the farms around the town were concerned, that was the way it should stay. Quiet. Peaceful. The kind of place people forced to work in the city moved to raise their kids. There was nothing wrong with Calhoun Corners and deep down inside Tia suspected Rayne had to know that, too.

As Tia watched Rayne's car disappear down Drew's lane, Drew bounded up the back steps of the wraparound porch and joined her. "What the hell did she want?"

Tia waved the marriage license. "The minister somehow took this with him."

Drew took the envelope, glanced inside and groaned. "Matt must have given him this envelope instead of the check for his services!"

"I'll take the check into town."

Drew shook his head. "Not alone. Not the day after our wedding. I'll get it to him tomorrow."

"But…"

"No buts. It might have appeared that Rayne came to drop this off, but you do realize she saw us apart, right?"

Tia's eyes narrowed. "You think she used our license as an excuse to spy on us?"

Drew laughed and shook his head. "You don't think she's going to come right out and tell you that she's here to see if we really are the happy couple we're supposed to be. The reverend probably mentioned that Matt had given him the wrong envelope and she probably volunteered to bring it out. Tia, I know you were friends in high school, but she's not the same Rayne anymore."

Tia nodded her understanding. It was just one more stupid thing she had done this weekend. But in a way, she was glad Rayne had showed up because now that she was angry she wasn't going to make another mistake. She would carry this charade through without a hitch.

* * *

Drew's stomach tied in a knot when he entered his dining room that evening. Mrs. Hernandez was serving dinner on the shiny mahogany table, which she'd set with the good china and crystal that she'd bought for him. She had flowers in the center of the table—roses, for which he'd probably get the bill. As he walked in, she was pouring a glass of champagne at his place setting. Tia's glass was already filled and he noticed the open bottle of sparkling grape juice sitting in the ice bucket.

"This is nice," he said, trying not to grit his teeth. This was hell. Seeing that Tia hadn't just brought her things into his room, but had been smart enough to put her clothes into empty drawers in his closet and her toothbrush beside his in the container on the sink had set his blood humming. If Mrs. Hernandez weren't around, he could ignore Tia, or insult her into ignoring him. Instead, he had to play a love-struck newlywed.

"Isn't it beautiful?" Tia said happily as she tipped her face up to his to accept his kiss. He gave her a quick kiss, but realized that as a newlywed he had to do better than a peck on her lips, and he deepened the kiss, sending his hormones into overdrive and making him tense enough to want to choke somebody.

"It *is* beautiful," he said, then turned to Mrs. Hernandez with a smile. "And you aren't needed." He didn't have to work to make his voice sound sex-starved and like that of a man hungry for his new bride. The kiss had accomplished that.

Drew's housekeeper smiled dreamily. "If you were

on a real honeymoon, you would be in a restaurant and you would have a waitress. Just think of me that way."

"If we were on a real honeymoon, we'd get room service. Now scram."

Huffing indignantly, but obviously realizing he was correct, Mrs. Hernandez shuffled from the room.

Drew took his seat at the head of the table. Sitting catty-cornered from him, Tia leaned forward and whispered, "Wasn't this sweet of her?"

"Or she's trying to trip us up as much as Rayne is."

Tia gasped. "But why? I might believe Rayne would be doing it because she likes Auggie Malloy and wants to see him get elected. But Mrs. Hernandez has no reason."

"To her it would be pure sport."

"But she likes me."

"Of course she does. My guess is she thinks I cast an evil spell on you and it's her job to rescue you."

Tia laughed, then turned her attention to filling her plate. They ate their dinner in almost complete silence until Drew realized that newlyweds would be chatting and flirting. He leaned toward Tia and whispered, "Giggle."

She peered at him. "Giggle?"

"Make it sound like I said something cute."

Tia whispered, "I'm not going to giggle. I don't giggle."

Deciding that all their whispering could pass as lover's communication, Drew kept it going. "Past the giggling stage, huh?"

"Long ago."

"I know," Drew admitted, continuing to keep his voice soft and quiet, particularly since the mood was right for him to do something that had been gnawing at him since he'd talked to Tia's dad the day before. "I think I need to apologize."

She tilted her head questioningly. "Apologize?"

"You really have grown up. You're not a kid. You're twenty-four. Lots of women have six kids by now."

She laughed.

"Good enough." When Tia gave him a confused look, he said, "The laugh. If Mrs. H. was listening at the door, your laugh would have made her think I said something clever."

"Oh."

The candles around the roses sent light flickering across Tia's face. Brimming with confusion, her eyes told him she was as unsure as he was, and that made him want to comfort her. Thinking of comforting her made him want to hold her. And, of course, thinking of holding her made him want to make love. In his head, Drew cursed Mrs. Hernandez, who was probably standing just beyond the swinging door, then he cursed himself for being so spoiled as to employ a full-time housekeeper.

"Maybe I should fire her."

"Oh, no! Don't do that!"

"Tia, it's only because she's here that we have to sleep together."

"I thought you were sleeping on the floor."

Great. "Yeah, that's right. I said that."

She shook her head. "It really doesn't matter since I'm leaving tonight."

"You're leaving tonight?"

"I have to be at work bright and early tomorrow. About an hour ago I realized it would be smarter for me to leave as soon as we finished dinner, rather than try to get up early enough to drive in the morning."

"Oh." All Drew's hormones dropped dead as if they'd been shot. "Oh," he said again, not nearly as concerned with his dearly departed hormones as he was with the disappointment that spiraled through him. "I didn't realize you had to leave so soon."

"The campaign that kept me in Pittsburgh for the past two weeks hasn't been redone yet."

He couldn't complain about her failed campaign since it had saved them from spending two long weekends together before their wedding, when they could have slipped up. It had also saved them from taking a fake honeymoon. He should be applauding it. He should not feel disappointed.

"So, does this mean you can't come home next weekend?"

"No. We now have a new concept for the cereal account. The team leader has already run it by Mr. Barrington, who sort of growled his approval." She grimaced. "There'll be no surprises in our presentation, but also no big failure, either. The point is, I'll be able to come home on weekends." She peeked at him. "That is, if you think it's a good idea."

"Considering that we aren't taking a honeymoon, I think it might look suspicious if you don't."

"Me, too." She glanced down at her cleaned plate, as

OFFICIAL OPINION POLL

ANSWER 3 QUESTIONS AND WE'LL SEND YOU
2 FREE BOOKS AND A FREE GIFT!

0074823 |||||||||||| |||| |||| ||||||||

FREE GIFT CLAIM # 3953

YOUR OPINION COUNTS!

Please check TRUE or FALSE below to express your opinion about the following statements:

Q1 Do you believe in "true love"?

"TRUE LOVE HAPPENS ONLY ONCE IN A LIFETIME."
○ TRUE
○ FALSE

Q2 Do you think marriage has any value in today's world?

"YOU CAN BE TOTALLY COMMITTED TO SOMEONE WITHOUT BEING MARRIED."
○ TRUE
○ FALSE

Q3 What kind of books do you enjoy?

"A GREAT NOVEL MUST HAVE A HAPPY ENDING."
○ TRUE
○ FALSE

YES, I have scratched the area below.

Please send me the 2 **FREE BOOKS** and **FREE GIFT** for which I qualify. I understand I am under no obligation to purchase any books, as explained on the back of this card.

310 SDL EFZJ

210 SDL EFX7

FIRST NAME

LAST NAME

ADDRESS

APT.#

CITY

STATE/PROV.

ZIP/POSTAL CODE

www.eHarlequin.com

(STF-R-06/06)

DETACH AND MAIL CARD TODAY!

The Silhouette Reader Service™—Here's How It Works:

Accepting your 2 free books and mystery gift places you under no obligation to buy anything. You may keep the books and gift and return the shipping statement marked "cancel." If you do not cancel, about a month later we'll send you 4 additional books and bill you just $3.57 each in the U.S., or $4.05 each in Canada, plus 25¢ shipping & handling per book and applicable taxes if any.* That's the complete price and – compared to cover prices of $4.25 each in the U.S., and $4.99 each in Canada – it's quite a bargain! You may cancel at any time, but if you choose to continue, every month we'll send you 4 more books which you may either purchase at the discount price or return to us and cancel your subscription.

*Terms and prices subject to change without notice. Sales tax applicable in N.Y. Canadian residents will be charged applicable provincial taxes and GST.

If offer card is missing write to: Silhouette Reader Service, 3010 Walden Ave., P.O. Box 1867, Buffalo NY 14240-1867

BUSINESS REPLY MAIL
FIRST-CLASS MAIL   PERMIT NO. 717-003   BUFFALO, NY

POSTAGE WILL BE PAID BY ADDRESSEE

SILHOUETTE READER SERVICE
3010 WALDEN AVE
PO BOX 1867
BUFFALO NY 14240-9952

NO POSTAGE
NECESSARY
IF MAILED
IN THE
UNITED STATES

if finally realizing she'd finished eating. "So, I guess I'll just go upstairs and get my makeup case."

"Great."

"I'll leave my other things here…in the drawers. Since I'll be back next week."

"Fine."

"Okay."

She rose and left the room and when the door swung closed behind her, Drew also rose and went to the foyer to wait for her. At first, he considered kissing her goodbye at the bottom of the steps, putting on something of a show for Mrs. Hernandez, but his heart wasn't in it. He scolded himself, once again reminding himself that he should not be disappointed because technically he was getting out of a long night of torture. But he *was* disappointed and he couldn't figure out why.

When she came downstairs, he walked her outside, across the porch and to her car. She tossed her makeup case onto the passenger's-side seat and said, "I'll see you Friday night."

He nodded. "Yeah."

"Just give me a quick kiss so I can get going."

The way she said that made his blood simmer. He knew this was a charade. He knew he shouldn't feel disappointed. He knew he should be glad to kiss her outside, in the dim glow of the pole lamps he used to light the way to his garage and stables. He also knew he should be glad it could be a quick kiss, but he wasn't any of that. He didn't know what in the hell he was. But he wasn't glad. Not even a little bit.

In the end, he gave her the quick kiss, refusing to fall victim to the temptation of her mouth. He watched her drive down the lane, waving, and then stormed up to his room. He would shower, put on something comfortable and watch TV before going to bed and getting a decent night's sleep. If it killed him, he would be glad she was gone.

But the second he stepped into his room, he smelled her and he realized it was going to be a long night anyway. He reminded himself that if he made this marriage real the divorce would be much more painful, but it didn't help. He might have been able to use that line on himself before this, but tonight it didn't work. All he could think of was that she was his wife.

And she was already pregnant.

And he was having the devil's time convincing himself that he had to keep his hands off her.

Chapter Six

As Drew entered his kitchen the following Thursday morning, Mrs. Hernandez said, "I heard you walking around last night."

Heading for the breakfast nook, Drew said nothing. As far as he was concerned, his pacing around his house for the past four nights as if lost made perfect sense for a newlywed whose brand-new wife worked in another city. It made no sense at all for a man who wasn't supposed to want to be married. But that didn't matter. Mrs. Hernandez knew only the charade. So she should think his behavior normal.

"You know, if you wanted to, you could drive to Pittsburgh."

Halfway between the breakfast nook and the back door, Drew stopped dead in his tracks and faced Mrs. Hernandez. If he didn't at least address this, she'd nag him for the rest of the day. "Drive to Pittsburgh and do what?"

Mrs. Hernandez shrugged. "I don't know. Maybe just be there when she gets home?"

"She's busy, Mrs. Hernandez. She doesn't need me underfoot."

"Or maybe what she needs is a supportive husband waiting with dinner when she gets home?"

Drew squeezed his eyes shut in frustration. She had him. There was no way he could win this argument. Any reason he gave for staying home made him look like a bad husband. At the same time, he couldn't actually go to Pittsburgh and be at Tia's house tonight. Talk about a way to give his pretend wife all the wrong ideas. Tia would only be hurt in this deal if he allowed her to get her hopes up that this marriage could become real. And she'd only think the marriage might become real if he started doing things to lead her to believe that. He couldn't make a surprise trip to Pittsburgh.

Instead of continuing on to the breakfast nook, he walked to the front door and grabbed his hat. His only recourse was retreat. "I don't have time for breakfast."

"But—"

Drew opened the door and ran across his back porch and down the three steps to the sidewalk. It was a damned shame that a man's home ceased to be a haven. But his haven was now gone. Not only could he smell Tia in his bedroom and feel her presence in most of the other rooms of his house, but now Mrs. Hernandez was starting on him.

He jumped into his truck and drove to town. Too long before six o'clock in the morning for it to matter, he found himself on the threshold of the diner, about to pay for food that was probably going to waste on his kitchen counter.

Unfortunately, as he pulled open the diner door, he caught sight of Mark Fegan, Rayne's dad, sitting at a table in the back. He didn't recognize the man with Mark, but he didn't care. Running into Mark Fegan that morning would absolutely cap his bad mood and he didn't want that. Somehow or another, he wanted to put himself in a good mood. He wouldn't do that by staring at Mark Fegan the whole way through breakfast.

He backed himself out of the diner door and was about to turn to leave when he noticed Mark and his companion rise. If Drew had arrived two minutes later, he would have missed them. Which meant that if he stayed out of sight for the time it took Rayne's dad to pay his bill and leave, he could simply walk in and have the nice, peaceful breakfast he wanted.

He ducked into the space between the diner and the hardware store on the right, knowing that Mark's office was down the street to the left so he would be out of Mark's way. It took a minute before the diner door opened. Mark and his friend passed close by Drew as they made their way to a Chevy Suburban parked on the street in front of the diner.

"I'm not going to sugarcoat this," the balding, sixty-something man said. "The people I represent think you're failing them. Putting a few editorials on an op ed page might have made Capriotti look bad, but he isn't running scared, and nobody's talking about voting for Auggie Malloy in November."

Mark combed his fingers through his thinning brown hair. "Exactly what do you suggest I do?"

The man laughed. "Mark, you seem to keep forgetting that *you're* the one who promised he could get Capriotti out."

"I thought I could. But I got all the mileage I possibly could out of Ben's heart attack. Even casting aspersions on his sons didn't create enough stress to push him into bowing out of the race!" Mark countered angrily. "I can't start making things up."

"If you'd check on his daughter, you wouldn't have to make things up."

"Why? You think there's something noteworthy in her marriage?" He laughed. "She's had a crush on Drew Wallace since she was a kid." Drew rolled his eyes. Did everybody know that but him? "Their wedding wasn't a surprise to anybody."

"Her wedding might not be news, but I bet a few people might be surprised to hear Ben's brilliant daughter is on the brink of being fired."

Drew cursed under his breath.

But Mark looked at his companion as if he were crazy. "Exactly how can I use Ben's *daughter* getting fired to make *Ben* look bad?"

Mark's companion shook his head. "You said yourself, this isn't about reality, but about stress. Pushing Ben until he realizes he has a choice between the election and his health, and hoping he chooses his health."

"He's a lot stronger than I thought."

"That's not my problem. You're the one who said he could get Ben out. That was the deal you made, and I'm tired of holding your hand. You told us this would be easy. The next time I come back here, I won't be alone and the guys I'll bring with me won't take no for an answer on the money you owe them."

With that, the stranger jumped in his Suburban and sped off. Mark stared down the street after him for a few seconds, then blew out a frustrated sigh, turned and began walking down Main Street toward the newspaper offices.

Drew emerged slowly from the small space between the diner and hardware store. Mark wasn't flexing his journalistic muscles. This was serious. Not only did Mark Fegan owe money to the wrong people, but it sounded as if Auggie Malloy had probably agreed to change the ordinances or zoning laws necessary to allow an industrial development in Calhoun Corners. So somebody wanted Ben gone. Badly.

Drew removed his Stetson and combed his fingers through his hair. At least now he knew the reason Mark was trying to get Ben out of office. Even better than that, he knew that Mark had run out of ammunition—except for Tia's troubles. Though even Mark admitted he couldn't think of a way to spin that against Ben.

Drew was tempted to believe that Ben's problem with bad editorials was over, but his typical pragmatic intuition told him that he couldn't get too cocky. Mark could be pretty damned crafty if he wanted to be. Drew couldn't quiet the sixth sense telling him he couldn't let this loose end hang.

He smacked his hat against his thigh. Tia had given him the impression her failed cereal campaign was under control, and, since he didn't think she had lied, that could only mean there was something else going on, or maybe there was another aspect to her original problem. Something she didn't feel at liberty to confide. He could ask Ben and Elizabeth, but then they'd figure out that Drew and Tia never really talked, so that wouldn't work, either.

But even as he thought about talking to Ben and Elizabeth about their daughter, something else struck Drew. Though the vows he and Tia had spoken the Saturday before were supposed to be temporary, he felt a loyalty to his wife that couldn't be denied. He couldn't just go to her parents and ask them whether they knew she was about to be fired.

Of course, if he made a quick trip to Ben and Elizabeth's to say hello, Tia's troubles might come up naturally in conversation. If they did, then Drew could analyze whether there really was something to worry about and maybe get a head start on figuring out how to help fix whatever was wrong.

Drew turned away from the diner and toward his pickup. Ten minutes later he was driving down the Capriotti's lane. The sun was beginning to come up, so when Drew jumped out of his truck, he headed for the stables rather than the house. He found Ben standing by the corral with one booted foot on the bottom rung of the fence, watching a chestnut mare.

"Isn't she beautiful?"

Drew took in the horse's well-defined musculature and her shiny coat. "She's going to produce some terrific foals."

"If I can find the right stud, I'm thinking she might just produce my Triple Crown winner."

Drew whistled low. "You do have plans."

"A few," Ben said, turning to lean against the fence. "My kids are all gone now, settled. Unconventionally as it may be in Jericho and Rick's cases. The point is the kids are gone and I've got enough put away to live well." He shrugged. "I can take some risks."

Drew nodded.

"So what brings you by?" Ben asked.

Drew shrugged. "I don't know." He'd already decided he couldn't ask Ben directly if he knew what was going on with Tia at work, so Drew knew he had to wait for it to come up natuarlly. He grinned and punched Ben's arm. "I guess I missed you."

"Right," Ben scoffed. "You usually need something when you come over this early."

"Really?" Was he that selfish and that predictable?

"Yeah. So what is it?"

Knowing this was his opening to bring Tia into the conversation, Drew said the most logical thing, and hoped that Ben picked up the cue. "I guess I just miss Tia." He shrugged. "You know. Company."

Ben laughed. "I thought Mrs. Hernandez lived with you?"

"She's not really company. Tia doesn't talk my leg

off about stupidity, yell at me as if she's my mother or force me to eat vegetables." Even as he said that, Drew realized it was true. Tia was a very easy person to live with.

Ben laughed. "She's a quiet one," he agreed. "I think after hearing her two brothers constantly arguing, she decided to take one of life's easier paths. She hardly talks at all."

"No kidding," Drew said, frustrated, because if Ben's comment was anything to go by, Tia hadn't spoken to her father about her troubles, either.

"You two haven't hit a rough patch already?"

"No!" Drew protested. Realizing he'd spoken too strongly, he pulled in a quiet breath and said, "I just told you, I'm here because I miss her."

"Yeah," Ben said, glancing out at his horse again. "Tia's something special."

Drew might only be coming to realize that, but her dad had always thought so. Tia wouldn't spoil her dad's image of her by admitting to a job failure. Ben wasn't going to be able to help him.

"I guess I'll be heading home."

"Elizabeth has some pancakes."

Drew's stomach rumbled and he remembered he hadn't even had coffee yet. "That might be nice."

Ben slapped him on the back. "Let's go eat."

Drew followed Ben into his house, strictly for breakfast. If Tia hadn't spoken to her dad about her troubles, chances were she hadn't talked to her mother, either, if only because she wouldn't want her mother telling her dad.

He considered phoning her. But what would he say? "Hey, I just called because I heard somebody tell Mark Fegan this morning that you were about to be fired. So, what's up with your job?"

Yeah. She'd love that. He had to think of a way to approach her that wouldn't put her off or make her defensive, but would give her an opening to confess whatever problem she had so that he could help her fix it. Luckily, he still had all of today and Friday to think through how to do that.

He left Ben and Elizabeth's house after breakfast, knowing he was going back to a house that held too many memories. He smelled her in his bedroom, pictured her in his dining room and remembered kissing her in his kitchen.

He drove directly to his stable, wondering what the hell had happened to his safe, sane life, and knowing he wouldn't get even a piece of it back until after he and Tia divorced.

Somehow, that didn't comfort him the way it should.

Tia pulled her sports car into the driveway of Drew's house Friday night, exhausted because her troubles at work had turned into an out-and-out war. The week had begun normally enough. She had been assigned projects and tasks, but when she tried to ask questions of the staff members who were normally very happy to work with her, nobody would speak to her. At one point, she had stood in the center of their circle of desks frustrated and flabbergasted that in three days nobody had as much as said good morning, and she noticed Glenn Olsen watching her, smirking.

It didn't take her genius-level IQ to deduce that Glenn, who was next in line for a promotion and who believed management had hired Tia to groom her to take one of the executive-level positions he'd been working for, wanted her out. In fact, when she thought back to how easily he had accepted her idea for the Barrington Cereal campaign she could kick herself for not seeing he was setting her up. Because her idea had failed, she was responsible for the entire team having to redo one ad campaign while also working on their regularly scheduled project. He hadn't simply found an avenue to make her look unqualified; he'd found a way to get the other members of her team so angry with her they were freezing her out. Right now, for all intents and purposes, she appeared to be a stupid woman who couldn't work with people.

Tired and feeling as defeated as a person could feel, Tia opened the front door of Drew's house and set her suitcase in the foyer. As she straightened up from dropping her bag, she was enfolded in a bone-crushing hug.

Mrs. Hernandez squeezed her twice, then let her go and immediately began fussing. "Why are you late? Have you had dinner?" She pushed Tia away and took a long look at her. "Have you eaten at all this week?" She peered at her face. "Are you sleeping?"

"Let her alone, Mrs. Hernandez."

Drew's voice from the living room doorway caused Tia's heart to stutter. She didn't want to believe that she was coming to like seeing him too much, so she convinced herself she was so desperate to be in the company of anybody not trying to get her fired that even he would do.

But when she turned to smile at him and he caught her gaze, liquid warmth flooded her. His thick dark hair curled around his face, which was tanned from hours in the sun. His wonderful wide shoulders and muscled chest stretched his T-shirt to its limits. He was so darned good-looking and so darned strong that part of Tia wanted to simply sink against him and weep with gratitude that she was finally home.

Before she could remind herself that this wasn't really her home, he crossed the foyer to her, wrapped one arm around her waist and pulled her to him for a kiss, and Tia melted. The feeling of his lips against hers sent blood coursing through her veins at the same time that it seemed to liquefy her bones. She slid her arms around him, enjoying the kiss, believing he really had missed her and allowing herself the tiniest of concessions that she had missed him, too, until he whispered, "We need to talk."

Then she knew that hugging her to him and kissing her was a way to get them close enough that he could tell her they needed some time away from Mrs. Hernandez.

Disappointment spiraled through her, but she pulled away from him with a sunny smile, not about to let this part of her life get as far out of control as her work life had suddenly become. "I missed you, too." She looked at Mrs. H. "Both of you."

"Well, of course, you missed *me,*" Mrs. Hernandez

said, grabbing her arm and leading her toward the kitchen. "You need some food!"

"Mrs. Hernandez, really, Tia and I would like some alone time."

"Get your mind out of your hormones, Mr. Wallace," Mrs. Hernandez said. "I need to feed this girl."

Tia shot him a helpless look as Mrs. Hernandez dragged her to the kitchen, but the truth was she didn't mind being dragged away from him. She wasn't in the mood to hear more bad news. She wasn't in the mood for another problem. She decided to subtly tell Drew to hold off on the need-to-talk discussion until tomorrow. After a night's rest she was sure she would be able to take on something else.

He played right into her hands by following her into the kitchen.

Walking to the round oak table in the breakfast nook, she said, "Actually, Drew, I'm not just hungry. I'm also tired."

"See?" Mrs. Hernandez said smugly. "She's not in the mood for your *alone time*."

"Mrs. Hernandez!" Tia gasped.

"Yeah, Mrs. Hernandez," Drew said. "Did you ever stop to think that when I said alone time, I wasn't referring to sex, but I wanted time to talk to my wife without you listening?"

"No, I didn't think that. And do you know why? Because I know you. When you find something you like you're obsessive."

"Whatever," Drew said, obviously deciding there was

no point in arguing with his housekeeper as he took a seat at the table.

Mrs. Hernandez turned her attention to Tia. "I've got spaghetti that I made for Drew tonight," she said, rattling off supper choices for Tia. "It's still warm. But I also have leftover meat loaf from yesterday and some roast beef from the day before."

"Okay."

"Okay?" Mrs. Hernandez frowned. "Which one did you want?"

"All of them."

"All of them?" Mrs. Hernandez parroted, still confused.

Tia smiled. "Yeah. All of them."

Drew burst out laughing as Mrs. Hernandez hurried away. Getting the plate of spaghetti and warming the meat loaf and roast beef should keep his nosy house-keeper busy for a while.

He caught Tia's gaze. "We really do need to talk."

"Honestly, Drew, I'm tired."

Drew smiled sympathetically, but inside he was re-joicing. Though Tia didn't know it, she'd just handed him the perfect opportunity to get her to spill her guts without looking obvious. "What has you so tired?"

"Work. And I'm not in the mood to talk about it and I'm too tired to hear about any other troubles we have." She cast a pleading look in his direction. "I just want about sixteen hours of sleep. Tomorrow I'll deal with everything you feel needs attention."

He took a breath. So much for thinking she'd spill her

guts. But with Mrs. Hernandez returning soon, he decided not to argue.

His housekeeper eventually bustled back with a plate of spaghetti. "Eat this, first. Lots of carbs. It will give you energy." She smiled benignly at Tia, then turned to Drew. "You know, Mr. Drew, a gentleman would respect his wife being tired."

Drew shook his head. Why couldn't Mrs. Hernandez's sister have needed another month or so of care? "I do respect my wife," he began, but Mrs. Hernandez cut him off.

"Then you should sleep in the guest room."

"The guest room?" Drew blurted, not sure if she'd given him a reprieve or completely ruined his plan. Not sleeping in the same room with this sweet-smelling woman he couldn't have was like a gift from God, but he needed to get her work story out of her. On top of that, it would look odd for him and Tia to sleep apart for any reason. They were supposed to be madly in love. If she was tired, he was supposed to comfort her. And that, he decided, was his ace in the hole. She was tired. What would a normal guy do with a normal pregnant wife who was tired?

It was times like this he wished he were normal.

"Now why would I want to sleep apart from my wife," he asked, catching Tia's hand, "when it's obvious that she needs a little TLC?"

"I know all about your TLC," Mrs. Hernandez shot back. "You forget how long I've lived here and how many women I've seen sneaking down the front steps at dawn."

Drew barely stopped himself from cursing under his breath. This woman was going to be the death of him. "Tia knows she doesn't have to worry about me not respecting the fact that she's tired. I like her for more than her... Well, you know."

Though Mrs. Hernandez tossed him a skeptical look, Drew realized he'd meant that. He *did* like Tia. And not just for sex. Their relationship might have started with a burst of passion, but in the past few weeks he'd discovered Tia was a good person, obviously a strong-willed person if she was having a serious work problem that she hadn't shared with anybody, but nonetheless a good person.

Drew's feelings must have shown on his face because Tia smiled at him, then at Mrs. Hernandez. "He's right. I don't have to worry about him. Really, Mrs. H., I'll be fine."

Mrs. Hernandez harrumphed and walked back to the work area of the kitchen.

Drew studied Tia for a second, then said, "You do realize that we just blew our big chance not to have to sleep in the same room tonight."

Tia shook her head. "Not really. Mrs. Hernandez might be bulldozing for me to sleep alone, but in the morning, after some time to think about it, she'd realize it was odd for me not to want to sleep with you. We're madly in love, remember? I have to look like I missed you this week."

Their gazes met and clung with that sentiment hanging in the air between them. Something stirred in

Drew's heart, but he ruthlessly squelched it. They had a problem to resolve and he had to have his wits about him to get her to trust him so she would confide in him.

But holding the gaze of her pretty blue eyes, feeling the powerful sexual attraction that arched between them and remembering how open and trusting she'd been the day they'd made love, he suddenly realized that the best way to get her to trust him might be at his fingertips. All he had to do was seduce her. Give her the words of love she had so clearly wanted to hear, and she would be his. She would tell him whatever he wanted to know, and then he could solve the problem.

But then he'd give her all the wrong ideas, and when they divorced she'd be hurt.

He couldn't do it. No matter how much he needed to know her work problem, he wouldn't use how she felt about him. There had to be another way.

It might simply take him a while to think of it.

"And here's the meat loaf," Mrs. Hernandez sang, bringing a second platter to the table.

"Great," Tia said, eagerly spearing a slice the second Mrs. Hernandez set down the platter.

Though Drew normally never told anyone but Ben much about his farm, his horses or the disagreements he had with employees, he needed to do his part to fool Mrs. Hernandez. So, strictly for the sake of the charade, he began telling Tia the details of his own somewhat miserable week, but he unexpectedly recognized that opening up to her might be his alternative to using her feelings for him to get her to trust him.

So he talked. He told her absolutely everything that had happened that week, going on even after Mrs. Hernandez left the kitchen. Tia didn't seem to notice that with the housekeeper gone they didn't need to talk anymore. She listened to every word he said as if she really were his wife, until he noticed she was falling asleep at the table. Again, something twisted in his chest. Again, he ignored it. They couldn't afford to let feelings get in the way of their mission.

He grimaced. "Sorry about going on so long."

"That's okay," she said with a laugh. "That real conversation we just had will probably go a lot further to convince Mrs. H. we're legit than a hundred passionate kisses."

Drew laughed and rose from the table as Tia also rose.

"If you don't mind, I'm ready for bed."

He wasn't about to let her get away when they were talking so well. Any minute now he expected to be able to turn the tables and get her talking about her week, then her job, then whatever the hell was going on at that company of hers that was about to get her fired.

"I have to wake up early tomorrow, so I'll go with you."

She said, "Great," but there was an amazing lack of conviction in her voice.

Drew chuckled. "I thought you told Mrs. H. you trusted me."

"I do."

"Okay, then, loosen up," he said, directing her to walk before him through the hall and up the stairway. "Your shoulders are so tight I'm afraid they're going to snap."

She smiled weakly, but didn't really reply. Instead,

she climbed the steps and headed down the hall, hesitating at his bedroom door.

He reached over her shoulder and pushed it open, thinking she might simply feel odd about taking the liberty of walking into his room. But he knew it was more than that when he had to nudge her inside.

"I've got a sleeping bag," he assured her. "So it's not like we'll be sleeping together. We're just going to be in the same room. That's all." Then quickly, before she had a chance to think about what he'd said, he added, "Want the bathroom first?"

She demurely accepted, and left him alone in the big bedroom.

Drew walked to his closet where he'd stowed his sleeping bag that afternoon. As he got it out and unrolled it, he heard the sound of the shower and he frowned. He'd thought five minutes in the bathroom wouldn't be enough for their conversation to lose momentum, but apparently her bedtime ritual was a lot more complicated than his was.

Of course, she might have a point about needing to at least rinse off before bed. He had showered when he came in for the day, but it was a hot summer.

He sighed. All right. He would be considerate and shower, too. But he couldn't afford for her to fall asleep while he was gone, so he grabbed one of the spare master bath towels along with his robe, raced across the hall, showered and brushed his teeth. He also tidied up the bathroom and brought the dirty towel with him.

When he returned to the bedroom, Tia was already

in bed, but she wasn't settled. She shifted to the right, then the left, then rose up and punched her pillow. "I can't get comfortable."

"You just need to unwind."

"Right."

"Really. You look about as tense as a person can get."

She sighed. "It has been a long week."

Deciding this was his opening, he strolled across the room to his sleeping bag. "So, why don't you tell me what's going on at work?"

"Work?"

"Sure. You keep saying you're tired and it's been a long week." He shrugged. "I figure something must have happened at work."

"It's really not a big deal."

Keeping up the appearance of nonchalance so she'd relax and talk, he peered down at his sleeping bag. "Sounds like the perfect thing to talk about, then."

She sat up on the bed. "I don't feel right making you sleep on the floor."

He glanced over. Did she think he was so stupid he wouldn't notice she'd changed the subject? "I don't feel right that I told you every damned thing that went on in my life this week and you won't even confide one little work problem."

She took a breath.

He lifted the corner of the sleeping bag and lowered himself inside, absolutely positive that her guilt over making him sleep on the floor would cause her to blurt her story. Instead, she turned off the light.

Damn it! He heard the swish and crunch of the covers, and stifled a groan. This was another one of those reasons he didn't get involved with women. He really had told her every single thing—well, except for overhearing that conversation between Mark Fegan and the stranger—that had happened in his week, and she couldn't even tell him about one simple problem.

And he was sleeping on the floor for her, for Pete's sake! Didn't the woman understand anything about guilt?

Suddenly, the light popped on again.

"This bed is huge! We'd never even touch accidentally."

Drew rolled his eyes. Great. She'd invite him into bed, but wouldn't tell him her work troubles.

"Go to sleep, Tia."

She turned off the light. He closed his eyes. Silence filled the room. But the quiet actually made things worse. He was sleeping on the floor. She wouldn't confide her problem. Hell, he felt like he really was married.

He moved about a bit, trying to get comfortable, but he wasn't the slightest bit tired. The thick sleeping bag didn't do much to soften the hardwood beneath it. Thoughts of a new mayor, somebody who'd overturn or rewrite zoning ordinances that had kept Calhoun Corners a quiet little town for generations danced through his head. He could hear his sheets crackle and crunch with the movement of Tia's body—her nice soft body against his super-soft satin sheets.

He sighed. Well, that just officially made his life miserable. He had three choices. Think about how hard his floor was. Worry about how a new mayor would probably change his peaceful town. Think about Tia's body shifting on his sheets.

This was going to be one long night.

"You remember the failed cereal campaign I told you about?"

Stunned when Tia's soft voice drifted down to him, Drew shifted to his side, facing the bed, and cautiously said, "Yeah."

"Well, it's not as cut-and-dried as I made out."

Careful, not wanting to put her off, he casually asked, "How so?"

"When I was hired there was a rumor that management brought me on board to be trained for senior management."

"Well, you *are* smart." Super-smart, if he remembered correctly.

"But that also means I'll ultimately be promoted over a lot of people. I knew some people weren't happy about that, but everything seemed to be working out okay. But this week when I couldn't even get anybody to tell me if the coffee was fresh, I realized that the team leader has been working to get me out from the beginning. And though I have no proof, it looks like I actually handed Glenn the way to get rid of me when I came up with the cereal campaign idea."

Drew sat up. "How's that?"

"Glenn's been a team leader for two years. Yet he let us run with an idea that failed. Not only that, but the whole time we were working on it, he kept praising me.

I thought he was really cool to give me the credit, but I think the real reason he did that was so everybody would remember it was my idea that failed so that when the extra work came down, everybody would know who to blame."

"You fell for the oldest trick in the book. He used your confidence to make you look stupid."

"Yeah. And now, nobody wants to work with me. And I almost get the impression he's created some kind of scheme to get me fired."

Of course he had. That was what men did when they were angry. They picked an enemy and annihilated him—or, as in this case, her.

Drew considered his course of action only a second, then asked, "How smart is this guy?"

"How *smart* is he?"

"Can you beat him? Should you really be his boss?"

"Yes. When I was hired Glenn supposedly went into the personnel office and complained that if they brought me in to groom me for management, they were passing over lots of other qualified people. Rumor has it he was told that nobody else had the business background that I have. Mrs. Montgomery, the HR coordinator, even gave him a list of college courses he needed to take to be in line for a management position."

Drew weeded through everything Tia had said and homed in on the most important point. "You have a business background?"

"I minored in business in college. Though I knew I wanted to go into advertising, I wasn't really sure what kinds of jobs were out there and I knew I might end up being a consultant or even starting my own company. So I knew I needed to know how to run a business. It's that knowledge that gives me my edge."

"Okay, you deserve to be trained for management, and Glenn still needs some education." He paused and thought for a second, then said, "Unfortunately, you can't call everybody together and just blurt that out as if you're on the network news. They might buy it, but they won't like it. So the only way to rescue yourself is to bring in an eager puppy."

"Bring in a dog?"

"No, an eager puppy. You need to talk to your personnel director and ask her to transfer in somebody from another department who likes you. Somebody whose very willingness to work with you will make it obvious that other people are refusing to. That puts the ball back in their court. If they continue to refuse to work with you, *they* look bad."

She crawled across the bed and looked down at him from the foot. "How am I going to get somebody transferred in? They might have hired me to groom me for the upper echelons, but I'm not in management now. In fact, I'm a peon. Nobody's going to transfer somebody into my department just because I ask!"

Drew held her gaze. "You're supposed to be a smart girl. It's all your parents ever bragged about. Now it's time to prove it."

Chapter Seven

When Tia arrived home the following Friday night, she felt far different than she had the week before. Instead of being upset and confused, she was focused and confident, brimming with energy and so darned happy she could have sung a number from the *Sound of Music*.

"Drew!" she yelled, dropping her suitcase in the foyer as she had done the Friday before. "Drew, I'm home!"

She glanced in the living room and didn't see him, then trotted down the hall to the kitchen, but he wasn't there, either. She froze, suddenly realizing that she expected him to be waiting for her like a real husband. All along, he'd said he didn't want to have too much of a part in her life, but when he'd worked so hard to get her to talk the week before and had even helped her strategize, she'd thought he'd changed his mind. No matter how subtly, this week she'd been thinking about him, missing him, even looking forward to telling him about her job. With him nowhere to be found when he knew exactly what time she came home Friday nights, it was clear she'd made a mistake. He hadn't meant anything personal the week before.

"I'm here," Drew called, jogging down the steps, and Tia's lungs inflated again.

Maybe she hadn't made a mistake? If the spring in his step was any indicator, he was eager to see her and hear her news.

"So? How did it go?"

"It was great!" she said, impulsively grabbing his biceps and stretching to her tiptoes to kiss him, if only to thank him. "Thanks to you!"

Drew beamed with pride. "My plan worked?"

"Not a hundred percent," Tia admitted with a grimace. "Glenn's still being a horrible pain in the butt. But the HR office sent up a real gem from the stenopool."

Drew's face twisted in confusion. "The stenopool?"

"Yes!" Tia said with a laugh. "I'll explain after I get something to eat. Is Mrs. Hernandez here?"

Drew sighed. "Do fish swim? She's been cooking all afternoon."

Tia squeezed her eyes shut in delighted anticipation. "Thank God. I'm starving."

"Good. We can eat together. I had a meeting tonight, so I missed dinner."

Drew put his arm around her shoulders and led her back down the hall to the swinging door into the kitchen.

And suddenly Tia felt as if she was home. Really home. After all the years of living in an apartment, she'd thought the new house she had bought would satisfy her feeling of loneliness, but it hadn't. Now she knew why. It wasn't a house that made a home, but people. Here she had a friend in Mrs. Hernandez and she and Drew were becoming more than friends. She almost hated letting herself believe that he liked her. But his eyes had absolutely glowed with joy when she'd told him about her job. He'd run down the stairs to see her and she'd driven like a bat out of hell to come home to him. Now, he had his arm around her. Was it too much to hope that they really were falling in love?

"There you are!" Mrs. Hernandez sang when Tia walked into the kitchen. She shuffled over and gave her a hug. "So, what are you hungry for?"

"What did you make me?"

"I was going to prepare a huge Mexican dinner for you," Mrs. Hernandez said, pulling out the kitchen chair for Tia to sit. "But I realized that might be a bit spicy. So I decided on a nice pot roast, fluffy mashed potatoes, glazed carrots and red velvet cake for dessert."

"Oh, Mrs. Hernandez," Tia said reverently. "That sounds fabulous."

"Do I get to eat, too?" Drew asked, walking to the chair across from Tia's.

"I suppose," Mrs. Hernandez said. "But you know, Mr. Drew, you look like you're putting on weight to me."

Drew laughed. "Not hardly."

"Really? Take a look at that belt."

Mrs. Hernandez walked away and Tia burst out laughing. Drew glanced down at his belt. "I'm not gaining weight."

Tia raised her hands in surrender. "Whatever you say."

Drew sighed as if put upon. "Let's get back to talking about your job. What about the woman you got from the stenopool?"

"Marian was divorced about eight years ago and she and her husband shared custody of her kids."

Mrs. Hernandez set a filled plate in front of Tia and Tia smiled up at her.

"Anyway, since she had a lot of time on her hands while her kids were with her ex, she decided to get a degree."

Drew nodded as Mrs. Hernandez put an empty plate in front of him, then set a bowl of mashed potatoes and a platter of roast beef in the center of the table.

"Remember, portion control, Mr. Drew," she said when she brought the gravy.

Drew scowled at her. Tia stifled a laugh, quickly getting back to her story. "She could only handle a few classes a semester, so it took her eight years to get her degree, but I'm telling you, it was worth it. With the experience she got working as a legal secretary and a secretary at a bank and secretary at an engineering firm, and then as a secretary with our ad firm, there isn't much this woman doesn't understand."

"So, with your brain and her experience you two are probably unbeatable."

"I don't know about unbeatable, but we click. And we had ideas bouncing around all over the place last week."

"Did having her around force the other members of your team to come around and work with you, too?"

"Sort of."

"Sort of?"

She shook her head. "Everybody's coming around, but slowly. I think that's normal, though. I realized this week that dealing with office politics is a reality of life. I got so accustomed to being praised for everything I did in high school and college that I forgot the real world doesn't work like that." She shrugged. "But I'm okay with it."

"Really?"

She nodded. "Yeah. I mean, nobody said it was going to be easy."

"Well, good for you," Mrs. Hernandez said, reaching between Tia and Drew to take the empty potato plate. She frowned at Drew, but said nothing.

Tia laughed. "How did things go here this week?" she asked, changing the subject.

"Great. I got a new mare," he said, so easily that if she hadn't glanced up at him with sincere interest in her blue eyes, he might have continued. But she did glance up. She smiled into his eyes. Not like somebody forced into a charade with him, but like somebody who really liked him. He pulled in a breath and sat back on his chair. "It's nothing."

"Sure it is," she countered, again easily. They were behaving like two friends and though last week he had needed to talk so she would become comfortable enough to tell him her troubles, now that her problem had been fixed they didn't need to be friends.

"Just eat," Drew said, turning to dig into his food. He focused his attention on the roast beef in front of him, refusing even to glance at Tia. He knew he'd see hurt in her eyes, but that hurt would be a lot worse if they got further involved and she got her hopes up and then they divorced anyway.

He also hadn't forgotten that they were about to become parents. Divorced parents. He didn't think she'd use their child as a weapon against him. But he didn't wish to endure an ugly scene every time he picked up or dropped off his little boy or girl. So, getting close was bad. Distance was good.

When he finished eating, he rose from his seat. "There are a few things I need to see to in the barn."

"Great," she said, dabbing her mouth with her napkin before rising, too. "I'll come with you. I'd like to see the mare."

He didn't even pause on his way to the door. "No. It's late. You go upstairs and get your shower. I'll see you when I'm done."

Drew managed to find things to occupy him for a full hour. When he returned to his house, it was dark and quiet. He breathed a sigh of relief, tossed his hat to the peg at the foot of the foyer stairs and tiptoed up the steps and down the hall to his bedroom.

Though the room was dark when he opened the bedroom door, he could make out Tia's small form, looking lost in his king-size bed. In order not to wake her, he didn't turn on a light but tiptoed to the bathroom, then changed his mind, grabbed a towel and his robe and headed across the hall where the noise of the shower wouldn't disturb her.

When he returned to the bedroom, he rummaged for a pair of sweatpants that he'd cut into shorts and unrolled his sleeping bag. Just as he prepared to lower himself to the sleeping bag, the lamp beside Tia clicked on.

"You can't sleep on the floor."

He sighed. He didn't want to sleep on the floor, but that didn't mean he couldn't do it. "Sure I can."

She flipped back the covers of his bed. "This bed is huge. You know it is. We're in no danger of touching."

He drew a quiet breath. She might be right about not touching, but he would smell her and then all his senses would be heightened and he'd get even less sleep than he got on this floor.

"No."

"Okay, then I'm going to sleep in one of the spare bedrooms."

She edged her legs out of the bed, slid her feet into slippers and headed for the door. Drew stood staring. Not because she had the audacity to leave, but because of what she was wearing. Oversize pink print boxer shorts clung precariously to her hipbones while a solid pink tank top mercilessly caressed her breasts.

He swallowed. "You can't."

"Mrs. Hernandez suggested it last weekend. She won't be surprised."

"No, but eventually she'll be confused." He sighed. "Come on, Tia. Go back to bed."

"No."

He knew from the stubborn set of her chin that she meant it.

"Damn it."

"Your only alternative is to get into the bed with me."

Drew stormed to his bed. "Fine. I'm tired. I'm done arguing."

He fell into bed and Tia slid into her place on the opposite side. At least three feet of mattress separated them.

"See," she said, "plenty of space."

"Right," he growled.

"And lots of emotional distance," she said as she flicked off the light.

He took a breath. He wouldn't touch that with a ten-foot fiberglass pole.

"Last week you were Mr. Talkative," she said, her voice tiptoeing into the dark bedroom. "This week I explained that your advice had worked, now you're done." She paused only a second before adding, "I might have needed help with that problem because I was too inexperienced to see what was going wrong, but I'm not stupid. I figured out that for some reason or another it was important to our situation for that problem to be solved. That's why you helped me. Now that it's solved, you're back to being grouchy with me again." He felt her flounce onto her side. "Well, fine. I can be grouchy, too."

He sighed. Damn woman. "I don't want you to be grouchy."

"No, you just don't want to be my friend." He felt her

sit up, then the light flicked on again. "Damn it, Drew. We're having a baby. For the rest of our lives we're connected. We can't be enemies."

Drew sat up, too. "Well, we can't exactly be friends."

She frowned. "Why not?"

"Because…" He paused, all his good reasoning going out of his head when he accidentally glanced down at her tank top. He jerked his gaze to her face again and forced the image of her perfect breasts out of his head. "Because men and women really can't be friends."

"That's a crock."

"Okay, how about this? We can't be friends because I learned from my failed relationship that the better we get along as a married couple, the happier we are, the *worse* our divorce will be."

Her frown deepened. "Really?"

"Why does that surprise you?"

"I think it's the fact that you were ever happy that surprises me."

He glared at her. "*That's* my point. Had I never been happy with my ex-wife, I could have walked away with my sanity." He paused to grimace. "I still would have lost all my money, but at least I wouldn't have been hurt."

"So what you're really saying is that you've decided that if you go into a relationship expecting it to fail, you won't get hurt."

He stared at her. "This isn't a real relationship."

She laughed. "You think not? Maybe it's time for me to tell *you* not to kid *yourself*. We are not going to live together for eight long months without forming some kind of bond."

"Guess again."

She sighed. "You're impossible."

"Yet another one of my points. The fact that I don't want a relationship with you has nothing to do with you and everything to do with me. I *am* impossible. My expectations are always high. I expect nothing but the best from myself, nothing but the best from my horses, nothing but total commitment and loyalty from my friends."

"And you don't get that back from women?"

"Isn't that what I've been saying all along?"

"So it *is* personal." She flicked off the light.

Getting angry now, because she was twisting everything he said, he turned on the lamp on his bedside table. "No. It is *not* personal. And even if you can somehow manipulate this to the point that you think it's personal, it's about me. My expectations."

She rolled to her side and pulled the cover over her shoulder. "That's a delicate way of saying no woman can ever meet your expectations. I get it, Drew. No need to insult me."

Drew stared at her. It was too late. He'd already insulted her. He could see it in the tightness in her shoulders and the way she held herself so rigid she looked as if she would crack if he touched her.

That caused a tightening in his chest that he didn't like. Mostly because it reminded him of his marriage. It brought to mind the one argument he remembered having with Sandy when she'd made him feel guilty for spending so much time at work, though he was earning the money that she happily spent.

He took a quick breath. Geez, *there* was a trip down memory lane he hadn't needed to take. *This* was why he didn't get involved with women. They reminded him of the other woman in his life and, frankly, he did not care to revisit that failure.

He turned off the light. No matter what Tia thought, he had made the right choice in forcing them to keep their distance.

He ignored the twisting feeling in his heart, the one that kept reminding him that he had hurt Tia. In the end she would thank him for not letting them get involved. They would leave this relationship as emotionlessly as they had entered it. He wouldn't lose a dime or spend any time wishing he'd done things differently. She wouldn't spend a year getting over him. Once he was out of her life, she'd probably find somebody who really could love her.

His gut twisted again, but this time it was with jealousy. He didn't like thinking of her with another man, but he had to be a realist. She was a beautiful woman. Smart. Funny. Somebody was going to snap her up. He squeezed his eyes shut at the unexpected pain that shot through him when he thought of her with another man.

No matter which road he took he was going to get hurt.

Drifting off to sleep, with her floral scent reminding him of how soft she was, how sweet she was and how much he genuinely liked her, he began to wonder if there was any way to protect them at all.

And if they were going to get hurt, anyway, if he was going to miss her when she was gone, get jealous when she found another man and spend a year getting over her…

Then why wasn't he taking advantage of having her with him now?

Chapter Eight

In the barn, things were simple and easy. So easy that as Drew strode past the stalls, listening to the noise of horses impatient to be outside and hands taking care of the morning routine, he forgot all about Tia. The surrounding sights and sounds blocked out the nearly sleepless night he had spent, holding himself rigid and hugging his side of the bed until he could legitimately escape.

For the next few hours, he buried himself first in barn chores, then telephone calls and accounting. But at noon, Tia showed up at his office door.

Wearing jeans and a T-shirt and smiling, she sauntered into his office. "Daddy called."

He tossed his pencil to his desk. Of course she was smiling. She'd gotten a good night's sleep. He'd heard every inhalation and exhalation of her deep, even breathing. Rested and relaxed, she had no idea how difficult the night had been for him.

She needed sleep, though. She was carrying his child. And he also couldn't be angry with her for being attractive. Sexy. So sweet-smelling that every time he breathed, his hormones sighed with delight.

He sucked in a quiet breath and tried to smile. The smile didn't work, but at least he sounded accommodating when he said, "What did your dad want?"

She grimaced. "He needs a favor. The party's hosting a chicken dinner at the fire hall tonight. He was supposed to speak, but he's got the flu."

Afraid of the worst, Drew asked, "Is he okay?"

"Yeah, he's fine. It really is just the flu, but that's part of the problem. He needs somebody to assure his voters that he really is fine and somebody to give his speech."

Drew's eyes widened. "Oh, no." No matter how much he wanted to do his fair share, this was the line he refused to cross. He was *not* speaking in front of a crowd. "I'm not filling in for him. I do not give speeches. It's why I won't be a best man for anyone. I can't even give a thirty-second toast!"

"He didn't ask you to speak. He asked me." She shrugged. "I've done it before. It's actually very simple. You go to a dinner, shake a lot of hands, compliment the cooks and then give about a fifteen-minute speech." She shrugged again. "Piece of cake."

Drew's eyes narrowed. "So why are you telling me?"

"Because you have to go with me."

"I thought you'd handled these things before?"

"I have, but I wasn't married then. Daddy said to make sure you go with me."

Drew sighed. "So everybody sees we're happily married."

"Come on, Drew. The day after we decided to do this, you dragged me into town for breakfast because you said we needed to get out among people and show everybody we were together. You can't be upset because my dad realized the same thing."

"I suppose not."

At his reply, she smiled. "Great. This doesn't even have to disturb what you had planned for the day. Just keep doing what you were doing and come up to the house in time to get ready. We don't have to be at the fire hall until seven."

With that, she pivoted and walked out the door and Drew frowned after her. An odd sensation shifted through him. He'd expected that she'd hunted him down to make him feel guilty for their argument the night before. Instead, she'd been nothing but considerate.

On top of that, buried in that conversation was the fact that she'd easily accepted giving her dad's speech and he suddenly realized that was how she did everything. Easily. Accommodatingly. Without either fanfare or grumbling. Not once in this charade had Tia as much as whispered a word of discontent. Not even over having to drive six hours every Friday and Sunday night to fulfill her end of it. She hadn't griped about driving or argued about doing something either Drew or her dad decided needed to be done.

His frown deepened. She was such an easy person to get along with that he was beginning to feel like a real jerk for always fighting her, mistrusting her and telling her what to do.

Tia and Drew arrived at the Calhoun Corners fire hall and Tia was immediately swallowed up in a throng of her father's supporters.

"We heard that your dad was sick," George Thompson said, leading her into the center of the circle of people who had gathered to share dinner and hear a few words from her dad. Tia didn't know if the dinner had been scheduled to assure her dad's supporters that everything was fine with their favorite candidate, or to assure Ben that his supporters still believed in him. But whatever the reason, Tia recognized it was her job to make sure everybody left this fire hall totally convinced her dad was strong enough to continue being mayor.

"Is your dad okay?" Mary Zupan asked.

Tia laughed lightly. "He's fine. He has a touch of the flu. That's all."

"I was worried that the editorials were finally getting to him," Tom Grattan, a tall, thin man in his late sixties said. "At our age, a body can't manage that much stress."

"Those editorials aren't affecting Ben," Drew said before Tia could speak. "He knows Fegan's just trying to rattle his cage, but he's not letting him."

Drew jumped into Tia's role as the one reassuring everybody that her dad was fine. But he was doing such a good job that Tia decided there was no reason to interrupt him. He was the one person in this town Tia knew beyond a shadow of a doubt believed in her dad. There was no one better to sing his praises.

"Ben's heart attack last year might have thrown him for a loop," Drew continued, "but he handled it. Sure, he takes medicine, but the mayor's job isn't that difficult as long as we keep the town small and safe, the way we all want it to be."

"I'll drink to that," Tom Grattan said, lifting his glass in salute.

As the crowd that had gathered around Tia laughed, Tia glanced at Drew and smiled. He smiled back and something inside Tia melted. He wasn't just a good-looking man. He wasn't just somebody to whom she was attracted. He wasn't even her Prince Charming. He was the most honest, loyal man she had ever met.

This was why she loved him, Tia thought, for the first time letting herself admit she really did love him. He had the courage of his convictions. If he committed to someone, he committed for life. Which was probably why his broken relationship had crushed him. He gave everything he had and expected everything in return. But he'd never gotten it.

It was no wonder he couldn't trust.

"It doesn't hurt that there was no editorial this week," Julie Jenkins said, interrupting Tia's thoughts.

She glanced at Julie, a forty-something housewife who loved to dabble in local politics.

"There was no editorial?" Tia asked, her gaze wandering back to catch Drew's. He shook his head slightly, telling her nothing had appeared in the paper that week, and she returned her gaze to Julie.

"No," Julie said. "It was the strangest thing. We were all geared up for something, because Rayne hadn't been around all week." She paused to grimace. "When Rayne's away, we know it's because she's out of town investigating something."

"What do you think she was investigating?" Tia asked, but Drew pushed his way through the crowd and caught Tia's arm.

"Who knows with Rayne?" he said, smiling at the people around her. "Let's forget about her tonight. I'm just glad there was no editorial."

Everyone in the circle around Tia laughed, but knowing Drew didn't do anything without a reason, Tia recognized that for Drew to get the subject dropped so quickly, something had happened with Rayne.

Drew said, "I hate to remind you all that most of us have to get up at the crack of dawn, but we do. So, what do you say we get this dinner moving?"

The cooks and servers scrambled back into the kitchen as the rally-goers found seats. Drew led Tia to the main table.

"Got your speech all ready?"

"Yeah." This wasn't the time or place to ask what he knew about Rayne. She wasn't sure he would tell her, anyway. But if she needed to use persuasion, it was better to do it in private. "I got the speech ready, though I don't think I'll need it. It sounds like you have everything under control."

"Don't I always?"

That was another reason she loved him. He took care of the people he felt were his responsibility. She couldn't think of another man who would have gone as far as Drew had for a mentor and friend. Drew hadn't batted an eye at marrying her to protect her father from additional stress when he already had enough.

"Yes. You do."

"Okay, then. Eat fast, give that speech and let's get the heck home. I'm tired."

Tia took the seat that would have been her father's and spent most of the dinner chatting with the people at the main table. But she continued thinking about Drew. When he'd stopped the conversation about Rayne and the editorials, it was obvious he had been protecting her, if only from questions she couldn't answer. She had also suspected he only withdrew from her when he felt they were getting too close. Which meant that maybe the emotions she was feeling weren't one-sided. Maybe he was coming to like her as much as she was beginning to like him.

Unfortunately, Tia recognized that if she believed that, then she also had to admit that his need to withdraw was a clear sign that though he might like her, he didn't trust her.

And after everything they'd been through, that made her angry. She was as loyal and trustworthy as he was. Maybe more so. If he loved her as passionately and as loyally as he'd loved his ex-wife, she would love him with every fiber of her being. They would be the happiest two people on the face of the earth.

But he didn't love her. Otherwise, he wouldn't keep pulling back. Or would he? It wasn't like they'd really been in a relationship since May, as they'd been pretending. They'd only spent two weekends together. Even a friendship between them was a new idea for Drew. She'd been mooning over him, pining for him, fantasizing about him since she was fourteen, but he hadn't even noticed she'd grown up until a few weeks ago. She supposed he had a right to need a little more time than she did to fall in love.

But if he would give her a sign, one solid indicator that his feelings for her could get beyond friendship, she wouldn't hesitate to take their relationship to the next level, because she had no doubt that if they slept together again, she could convince him to try this marriage for real, and if they tried this marriage for real, it would never end.

She wouldn't let it end.

After dinner, Tia gave the speech her father had written, letting everyone know she was saying everything her father would have said, then she shook a few more hands before she and Drew climbed into his Mercedes and headed back to his farm.

Sitting behind the wheel, lost in thought, Drew seemed to be ignoring her, making her wonder if she'd only imagined that his feelings for her were improving. She also hadn't forgotten that he apparently didn't trust her enough to share the information he had about Rayne and the editorials.

Since asking him about it was as good a way as any to break the oppressive quiet in the car, Tia said, "Something tells me you know more about the editorial situation than you let on."

Drew said nothing. Keeping his eyes focused on the road in front of them, he didn't even acknowledge that she'd spoken.

Tia smiled ruefully. "I always know when you're hiding something because you pretend you're not."

He peeked at her. "Huh?"

"You have this way about you when you know something that you think needs to stay a secret. You don't exactly play dumb. It's more like you downplay the situation. You did it with us. You did it with the pregnancy. Tonight, you did it with the editorials and dragging me away from the crowd before anybody could say too much about the fact that there was no editorial this week." She paused only a second before she added, "So, what do you know?"

He took a breath, then another. As if debating telling her. Tia nearly prodded him. She could easily give him the big reasons why she deserved to know everything he did. They were partners, and they were in this charade for *her* dad. So she had a right to know what he knew.

Instead, she stayed quiet because she saw an unexpected potential in his hesitation. If he could trust her with something not related to their relationship, then it would open the door for him to trust her about more personal things. But he had to take the step himself.

Finally he said, "I overheard Mark Fegan talking with somebody last week."

Overwhelmed with relief that he'd decided to trust her, Tia nonetheless tried to sound casual as she asked, "About my dad?"

"And other things."

"What other things?"

Drew stayed quiet for a few seconds, but eventually he blew his breath out in a long sigh and said, "From what I could gather, Mark owes the wrong people some money. He apparently made a deal that if they forgave his debt, he would get Auggie Malloy elected."

"Somebody wants to bring in an industrial development," Tia said dully. Politics in Calhoun Corners always came down to one simple issue. Whether or not to rezone certain lands. "And they need zoning ordinances changed."

"That's what it seems."

Tia pondered that for a second, then said, "What does that have to do with there not being an editorial last week?"

He glanced over at her. "I'm guessing last week's target editorial didn't pan out."

"What was he targeting?"

"It wasn't a what. It was a who."

"Okay then, *who* was he targeting?"

Again Drew hesitated, but again he seemed to decide to trust her. "You."

Tia gasped. "Me?"

"The guy with Mark knew you were on the verge of being fired. He told Mark to look in that direction. Mark said he couldn't make a connection between you getting fired and your dad's campaign, but that doesn't mean he didn't try. His goal here isn't to make voters think less of your dad, but to stress your dad enough that he'll bow out of the election. I'm sure if Mark knew what was going on, he would have printed it, hoping it would rattle your dad."

She inhaled a quick breath. "That's why you coached me about what to do last week."

Turning his car into the lane for his farm, Drew nodded.

Tia said nothing as he parked the car in his garage and came around to her door to help her out. She didn't know whether to be furious that Drew had manipulated her when he'd coached her without telling her why, or happy that tonight he had trusted her enough to tell her not just the easy parts of his story, but all of it.

When they entered the kitchen, Drew turned on the overhead light. "Want a snack?"

She shook her head. "It's late."

"Yeah. I'm beat. Let's just go to bed."

Tia led the way to the bedroom and this time didn't hesitate at the door. Walking up the stairs she had realized there was actually a third part to the situation with Drew. He hadn't merely trusted her with the information, he'd trusted her not to get angry when he admitted he'd poked his nose in her business without fully disclosing why.

If she made a big deal out of that, she'd break the very thin thread of trust he had that she could accept what he'd done without getting angry, and he'd pull back again.

So she couldn't be angry. She had to accept that last week he didn't trust her, but this week he did. And wasn't that what a relationship was all about? Steps.

Technically, tonight he'd taken a huge step. A leap of faith. She'd be a fool to destroy that.

Drew yanked off his tie the second they stepped into the bedroom. Totally unconcerned that she was in the room, he unbuttoned his shirt. Deciding to take her cue from him, and also knowing that this was more proof they were growing closer, Tia slipped out of her dress.

"You looked pretty tonight."

Standing by the bed in her slip, Tia turned and smiled. A compliment from him was new, too. Another step, maybe? "Thanks."

"Blue is a really good color for you."

"Blue is a really good color for anybody with blue eyes," Tia said with a laugh. She headed into the bathroom, deciding not to make an issue out of his attention or their various states of undress. If she was reading this situation correctly, Drew seemed to be taking steps by leaps and bounds tonight and if she let him alone, nature would probably take over.

She swallowed, remembering the last time they had let nature take over. The night they had met at the party in Pittsburgh, they had operated on nothing but instinct, and it had been glorious. And maybe that was exactly what they needed. To get back to basics. To instinct. To what had drawn them together in the first place.

She finished her bedtime routine quickly, slid into her pajamas and entered the bedroom at the same time Drew was coming in from his trek across the hall to use one of the other bathrooms.

She slid into bed on the left side.

He slid in on the right.

She drew in a long breath, but Drew was so still Tia wondered if he was even breathing at all.

"Drew?"

"Yeah?"

It seemed a shame that their forward progress had stopped. But Tia couldn't seem to think of anything to say to jump-start Mother Nature. When she tried, her mouth grew dry. Her palms grew sweaty. She couldn't even speak, let alone flirt, let alone try to initiate a conversation that might lead to cuddling or kissing or doing the things she wanted so desperately to do with him.

She pulled in another long breath, but she still couldn't think of anything. Since nothing was coming naturally to her, she wondered if maybe he wasn't the one who was supposed to make the next move. But when a full minute went by without him saying or doing anything, Tia knew the chance had passed.

Stifling a sigh, she whispered, "Good night."

For a beat of time, Tia was convinced he wasn't going to say anything. Then he softly said, "Good night," rolled over and clung to the edge of the mattress the way he had the night before.

And that was when she knew that if she was going to have a fighting chance of keeping this marriage, she would have to seduce him.

* * *

The tickling of sensuous satin against Drew's nose awakened him. He brushed it away, but the pleasure of touching something so smooth tempted his fingers and they paused long enough to sample the silken delight.

But just as he realized it was hair, not satin, enticing him to savor and fondle, he felt the perfect round bottom of his wife nestled against him. That was when he realized he was aroused to the point that if he didn't soon get out of this bed, he wasn't going to get out without doing what his body wanted to do.

He slid a few inches away from her, but Tia shifted in her sleep, positioning herself up against him again. The cotton of her soft boxer shorts cruised against his already super-sensitive skin, and his nerves tingled as his body tightened.

"Don't I even get a good-morning kiss?"

Her voice sounded sleepy and sexy, a purr that resonated through Drew. Right now his entire body was screaming for a kiss. But he knew as well as she probably did that they wouldn't stop with a kiss. He also knew that if they did what they both wanted to do, their lives would get a whole heck of a lot more complicated.

She stretched seductively against him. "One kiss?"

He fought not to squeeze his eyes shut in frustration. She'd see it as the sign of weakness that it was. And he could not be weak. He had to be strong.

Apparently tired of waiting for an answer, she twisted around to face him, stretched forward and touched her lips to his. Sensation sang through him.

Need and emotion melded into the same thing. Realizing he was drowning, Drew quickly pulled away.

But she smiled up at him. "Hi."

"Hi," he whispered, his voice husky with need. He had to get the hell out of this bed, and right now. Unfortunately, he could not seem to get any part of his body to agree with his brain.

"Can I get a hug now? Maybe a cuddle? Just for a minute?"

Drew's breath froze in his chest. The kiss was one thing. A cuddle would be quite another. Though it might seem less sexual, it was actually a sign of emotion, affection. And that was the last thing they needed right now. "No."

"Please?"

The breath he had been holding burst out in a sigh. She couldn't know how desperately he wanted to make love to her, otherwise she wouldn't ask.

"I read somewhere that babies can hear in the womb," she said, and Drew nearly groaned. Talking about the baby was like bringing out the big guns. "And that parental affection is good for the baby's psychological development."

"Read that in a book, huh?"

She smiled. "Actually, my mother did."

Great. She'd heard it from one of the people he admired most in the world.

She shifted closer. Of its own volition, his left arm slid beneath her, even as his right arm slid around her. She snuggled against him. He squeezed his eyes shut.

"Another kiss wouldn't be totally inappropriate right now."

"Yes, it would."

"No, it wouldn't," she said with a laugh, then tipped her face up to him.

Drew's entire body froze. The biggest problem he had with Tia was that he didn't *want* to resist her. Common sense told him he should. Her dad was his mentor. They didn't intend to make this marriage permanent. He was too old for her. She was too young for him. And he had already lost once at love. He couldn't trust. It wasn't in his genetic makeup. One of them or both of them would be hurt if they added making love to the mix.

He knew all this.

So why couldn't his body understand?

She smoothed her hand down his back. He slid his hand down her back, along the soft cotton of her tank top, mimicking her movement. The response of his body was very much like the response of her sports car when he inserted the key. It roared to life like a powerful engine and Drew knew that if he didn't get out of this bed immediately, he wasn't getting out.

He wasn't sure where he found the strength to shift away from her, but he did. Before he let himself think too long, he rolled out of bed.

"I'm getting a shower," he said, walking into the bathroom, not listening to any arguments she might make, not listening to the screaming protests of his hormones, but focused only on the cold water that would soon sluice over him.

Chapter Nine

At noon the following Friday, Drew began pacing his office in the barn, worrying about Tia's impending arrival that night. The charade had gotten so confused that he wasn't sure he could get it back to where it was supposed to be. Not only had he and Tia slept together but they'd also cuddled, like people who really cared about each other. Worse, they were confiding things. He had no clue why he'd told her about the conversation of Mark Fegan's he'd overheard, except that after realizing how much of the burden of the charade she carried without complaint, it had seemed like the right thing to do.

He was beginning to understand her, to like her and to care about her, and if he wasn't careful he would find himself head-first in another relationship. Another *marriage*. Except this time, if this divorce got ugly, as his other breakup had, he stood to lose a lot more than a business or even the love of his life. He would lose his mentor. Which meant losing his place in the community. Which meant starting over again.

No.

No.

Marriages failed. He had to remember that.

"Who are you talking to?"

Mortified that he might have said any of that out loud, Drew spun around to face Mrs. Hernandez and he relaxed. If she'd heard any of what he'd been thinking—or speaking—she'd have a much more smug expression. Instead, she only appeared confused.

"I was working out a problem with a horse."

"Well, your wife's on the phone," she said, handing him the portable.

He stared at her. "Why didn't you just buzz me?"

She shrugged. "I don't know."

Sighing, he grabbed the phone from her hand. He knew why she'd brought out the phone. She wanted to listen in. Scowling, he said, "Scram!" But when she turned to go, Drew realized he'd just found the way to handle Tia. Be rude. Tia never argued with his rudeness. She always gave him his space. Being rude was his best tool to keep them from getting close.

Lifting the receiver to his mouth, he growled, "Yeah. What do you want?"

But instead of Drew hearing a sharp intake of breath, Tia's musical laugh came through the receiver.

"Wow. You're chipper this afternoon."

"No, I'm not," he said, continuing to be as obnoxious as he could be, if only because that really was the right thing to do. It didn't matter how cute Tia was, how sweet she was or how nice it was to have her around, no marriage lasted. And when real marriages broke up, people got hurt. This time around the price was too high.

"Because I have a lot on my mind. In fact, you're keeping me from work right now."

"Well, I'm glad you're busy because I can't come home tonight."

"Good."

She laughed again. "Gee, Drew, thanks."

He rubbed his hand across the back of his neck. Why couldn't she get upset and hang up like a normal woman? "Look, Tia, I'm busy." That had been how he'd saved his sanity when his marriage hadn't worked out. He'd kept himself so occupied with this farm that he didn't have time to think about his pain and pretty soon it left, and the disappointment dimmed. The same formula would work right now to maintain some semblance of distance in this pretend marriage. He would work. He wouldn't be available. He would be crusty and grouchy and so damn mean she wouldn't want to be around him anymore.

"Your not coming home will actually help me out."

"Just what a girl wants to hear."

Her wistful voice didn't even pierce the armor of his determination. Particularly since he knew she would thank him later.

"Whatever. Look, I've got to go."

The sound of her disappointed sigh drifted through the phone line to him, but when she spoke, her voice was unexpectedly cheerful. "Okay."

He squeezed his eyes shut, internally begging God not to let her be nice to him when he needed for her to be angry with him. "I'll see you next weekend."

"Okay. Sure," she said, then disconnected the call.

Drew clicked off, too, and walked to his desk. Now that he didn't have to worry about her imminent arrival, his mind cleared quickly and he did the work that he was supposed to have done days ago. He finished faster than he'd anticipated and then noticed the portable phone was still on his desk. Grabbing it, he rose from his seat and marched from the barn to the house.

"So, she's staying in Pittsburgh this weekend," Mrs. Hernandez said as he walked through the door.

"Yep." Even she couldn't dampen his mood. Tia not coming home was a good thing and if nothing else, he was able to work again.

"And you're staying here."

"We both have work to do."

"What work do you have to do?"

Drew sighed. "Lots of stuff."

"Like what?"

Drew suddenly realized she was fishing. All along, she'd had her suspicions about this relationship. She also had card club with Elizabeth, who had been suspicious, too.

"I think Tia would enjoy a visit from you," Mrs. Hernandez said with a casual shrug, but Drew knew that any time she was too casual, she was going in for the kill. "In all the time you two have been together, you've never gone to see her. She only comes here."

Jackpot. She'd found the weak spot in their story. Happily spending weeks apart did not make them look like a love-struck couple. If he didn't go to Pittsburgh, Mrs. Hernandez would have all the ammo she needed to take to Elizabeth.

He considered the situation for only a second because he quickly realized that visiting Tia wouldn't be a problem. By being grouchy on the phone that afternoon he'd set the stage well enough that she wouldn't jump to the conclusion that he'd come because he wanted to be there. And once he explained why he'd driven up, she'd easily see his trip wasn't personal, but a necessity to stave off Mrs. Hernandez's questions.

"You know what, Mrs. Hernandez? You're right. There isn't any work here that's more important than Tia." He smiled at his housekeeper. "Maybe I'll just go upstairs, pack a bag and be on my way."

Deciding to really mess with her head, he added, "You can have the weekend off…with pay."

With that, he turned and left the room. He hadn't seen the look on her face, but he would bet it was priceless.

When Drew showed up at Tia's office that evening, no one was more surprised than Tia. Her coworkers Lou, Lily, Gina and Marian were very close seconds. Their mouths gaped when he stepped into the room.

"How do you do," he said as they stood, staring at

him. Frankly, Tia didn't blame them. That week, she'd told each of them privately that she'd gotten married and she'd also admitted to being pregnant. So they weren't so much surprised by his existence as by his appearance. In his tight jeans and the T-shirt that outlined his muscles and accented his height, he looked like the perfect, all-American male. His Stetson and fancy boots added to his allure, making him drip with sex appeal.

Lou was the first to recover and Tia suspected that was because after Marian had been added to their team, Glenn was mysteriously moved to another department and Lou was the lone male in the group. The women, Tia was sure, were still silently lusting.

"It's a pleasure to meet you," Lou said, shaking Drew's hand. "Tia's told me a lot about you."

"She has?" Marian and Gina said simultaneously.

"She has?" Drew asked with a laugh. "I didn't think there was that much to say about me."

"And you don't give me any more information than is necessary," Tia said, stretching on her tiptoes to kiss him. She didn't know why he was here, but she was glad that he had come. So glad, her heart sang. "But I'll get you to spill your life story eventually," she added before she gave him another kiss, this one long and lingering.

When she pulled away, Gina, Marian and Lily stared dreamily. Lou shook his head. "Want some privacy?"

"How about just a minute or two?" Tia suggested.

Lou walked to the conference room door and when no one followed him, he turned with a beleaguered sigh. "Come on, girls."

Gina, Lily and Marian all growled, but eventually left with Lou.

"Nice group," Drew said when Marian closed the door behind them. "You'd never know they gave you an ounce of trouble."

"That's because Glenn's gone."

He turned and grinned. "Really?"

"Yeah. The week after we got Marian, he was transferred."

Drew laughed. "Wow."

Tia walked over to him and put her arms around his neck. He stiffened, but Tia wasn't concerned. She knew from the way he'd resisted her in bed the Sunday morning before and from their phone conversation that afternoon that he didn't want to fall in love with her. But she also knew that he was breaking. There was something between them beyond chemistry. She would call it friendship, but it was something bigger than that. They were attracted to each other, partners saving her dad and about to be parents. They had more things to cement their commitment than any two people she knew. His having traveled six hours to see her proved they were headed in the right direction.

She stretched on her tiptoes to give him a hug, loving the feeling of him, loving the feeling of being pressed against him, loving the fact that she was allowed to do things like hug him. "I have a surprise for you."

Drew pulled out of her embrace and walked over to the coffee cart in the corner of the room. "Yeah, well, before you get too cozy, I want to tell you—"

"No! Me first!" she insisted, opening the file folder she had on top of her stack of projects, pulling out a sonogram picture and taking it to him. "It's our baby."

He stared at the black square for a few seconds then looked up at her. "Is he invisible?"

Tia laughed. "*She's* not invisible," she said, pointing at the shadowy figure, then she quickly looked to see the expression on Drew's face. But rather than the joy she expected, his eyes were filled with tears.

"It's a girl?" he whispered.

"Well, we're basing that solely on the fact that we haven't found a…well, you know, the extra-special guy equipment. The next time around, we might see it clearly and know we have a boy. But right now, it looks like a girl."

He swallowed.

She lightly punched his arm. "Hey! I thought this would make you happy."

"It does."

"So don't I get a hug?"

As if in a trance he looked up from the picture and stared at her. She waited for him to say something, but he didn't.

"You're stunned."

"I think this is the first time that it's all real for me."

Tia slid her arms around his neck. "Yeah. That was what I felt, too." With that, she rose to her tiptoes and kissed him soundly. His arms slowly came around her as he deepened the kiss. Again, Tia felt as if she were coming home, but she knew the value of strategic retreat. She'd loved him since she was fourteen, but for

Drew all this was happening very fast. She stepped back and walked to her seat at the conference table again to retrieve her house key from her purse.

"This is for my house." She handed the key to him, then scribbled directions on a piece of paper. "And here's how you get there, in case you forgot how we got there after the party."

Holding the sonogram picture in one hand and the keys and directions in another, he stared at her. She smiled at him. "I won't be more than another two hours. There are some takeout menus on the refrigerator. Order something about a half hour before I get home."

He nodded, then turned and left. Once she was sure he was gone, Tia did the happy dance.

Just as Tia had promised, a little less than two hours later, she was pulling her sports car into her driveway. Drew watched from behind a drape in her living room. Her house wasn't as well-decorated as his. He knew that was partly because she hadn't owned it long enough to do much and partly because she couldn't afford to do everything she wanted.

But he also couldn't discount a third possibility. Maybe she hadn't even begun decorating this house of hers because she didn't intend to. Though she'd never done anything overt, and he even considered that she might not realize she was doing anything at all, Drew knew Tia wanted their marriage to work. Forever.

She stepped into the front foyer calling, "Drew? Are you here?"

"Yeah," he said slowly, moving away from the drape.

She walked into the living room, tossed her briefcase to the sofa and immediately rose on tiptoes to kiss him. Nature took over before common sense could take root, and Drew found himself kissing her back. Enjoying every sensation. Every second, until something amazing occurred to him.

He wanted this. All of it. A happy home. A beautiful woman who could be his friend as well as his lover. Children. Grandchildren.

He wanted everything he had lost with Sandy.

Worse, he liked Tia more than he had ever liked Sandy. He'd *adored* Sandy, and though that seemed like a stronger emotion, this friendly feeling was worse. He could see Tia fitting into his everyday life. He could see their little girl at his farm, playing in the lush green yard and learning to ride. He could see himself and Tia growing old. Making love. Laughing. Teasing. Just plain enjoying each other.

His heart squeezed in his chest. He could see it because he wanted it. No, he didn't just want it; he longed for it. He ached for it. He was a thirty-six-year-old man who had nothing in his life. Sure, he was successful, and, yes, he had friends, but they were nothing like the promise of a family. His family. A spouse. Children.

But he also knew how much it hurt when the dream died. He knew what it felt like to have your heart ripped out of your chest and stomped on. He knew how much it hurt when you realized the person you loved no longer loved you.

Forcing himself to remember every detail of the pain of Sandy's betrayal, then the pain of loneliness that had followed her betrayal and then the pain of not being able to move on for years, Drew swallowed. "I never unpacked."

Tia laughed and hugged him. "I didn't think you had. I know you probably have to go home tomorrow…"

"I'm going home right now." He stepped away. "Not only am I going home but I don't want you to come back to my house anymore."

"What?"

"Tia, I'm not dumb and I don't think you think I am. You've got to know I can see us growing closer."

"Some people would think that was a good thing."

"Not me. And not just because I'm twelve years older than you are, not just because your dad is my mentor and I don't want him to hate me after we divorce, but because I like you."

Tia shook her head. "Drew, liking me is good."

"Yeah, liking you is good because that's what has kept me from taking what you're offering. I could have happily slept with you Sunday morning. I could have easily fallen into step with enjoying being your husband. Hell, just now, I realized how desperately I want kids and a family…and I could use you to get those. But I won't, because I like you."

"You're not making any sense."

"Okay, then I'll spell it out. Relationships end. Spouses cheat. Lovers can't always handle it when everything doesn't go exactly as they'd hoped or planned.

And life is messy. Over the course of the next few years, something will happen to split us up. I won't hurt you like that, Tia."

"Do you hear what you're saying? You're saying you're sure we're not going to work out, and I don't believe that's true."

"Because you're young. You're not naive, but you're hopeful. I've seen enough of life to know that we have too many strikes against us. I'm too old for you. You're too nice for me. But even beyond all of those… Tia, you work six hours away from where I live. How do you plan to keep your job and live with me? You can't quit. You've worked too long and too hard to get where you are. There is absolutely no way this marriage can work."

"Drew…"

"No!" He said it more harshly than he'd intended, and when he saw the stricken look that came to her eyes it actually hurt him. But to Drew that was simply another confirmation that they'd let this go too far.

"Look, I figured it all out while you were still at work. I'm a bastard. Nobody would have even the slightest problem believing that I hurt you enough, ignored you enough or was just plain mean enough that you couldn't handle it."

"But—"

"You're off the hook!" Drew shouted, again more harshly than he'd intended, but he couldn't help himself. He felt like a caged animal that couldn't get free. Because she was the one holding him back, she was the one getting the brunt of his anger.

"Life is not a fairy tale. It infuriates me that you think it is. I've been patient. I've not taken advantage of you. But if you don't get out of my way and let me go, I will sue for custody of the baby."

Chapter Ten

Despite Drew telling her not to come to his home anymore, Tia arrived at his farm the following Friday, anyway. She opened the door, slid inside and set her travel case on the foyer floor as she always did. He'd said the charade was over. He'd said he didn't want her to come to his house. He'd said that he didn't want her in his life. And that had darned near killed her. But eventually she had put her own emotions aside and realized she'd heard fear in his voice.

Once she reminded herself of his failed relationship, she chastised herself for not recognizing sooner that this would happen. Of course, he was afraid. Of course, he'd barked at her, not bared his soul, telling her all his fears and vulnerabilities. Drew wasn't the kind of man to admit weakness. He would try to keep control, even if it hurt him to do so. Especially if he believed he was protecting her. And he did feel he was protecting her. He'd come right out and said it.

Which was exactly why she was here. She needed to prove to him that he wasn't protecting her, but hurting her by ending their marriage. Somehow over this weekend, she had to make him see that rather than dissolve the marriage before they got hurt, they needed to promise each other they would stick it out forever. Because that, she realized, was the real bottom line. If she could get him to promise never to hurt her, he wouldn't. He was a man of his word. And if she could get him to believe she wouldn't ever hurt him, he wouldn't go back on that conviction, either, because Drew had proved time and time again that once he put faith in someone, he kept it there— until that person gave him reason to doubt. And since she never intended to hurt him, desert him or even let him be unhappy, they would be fine.

Now, all she had to do was get him to believe it.

Straightening her shoulders and preparing for the fight of her life, Tia called, "Drew?"

When he didn't answer, she leaned against the newel post and called up the steps, "Drew?"

Again, no reply. The swinging door at the end of the hall opened and she eagerly glanced down the corridor, but it was Mrs. Hernandez, not Drew, who came scurrying up the hall.

"Miss Tia."

Tia took a long breath. "Uh-oh. Something's wrong. You've never called me Miss Tia."

Mrs. Hernandez smiled weakly. "Why don't you let me give you a little supper while we talk?"

Tia shook her head. "No. I know what you're going to say." She sucked in another quick breath. "He's not here, is he?"

"No."

Tia glanced around. "Well, maybe I'll just wait for him, then."

"You'll be waiting until next Tuesday."

"Next Tuesday?"

"I found his itinerary."

"Itinerary?"

"His flight schedule and hotel accommodations. He's on vacation." She paused and added, "In the Bahamas."

"I see." He'd probably come home right after he'd broken up with her and called his travel agent. So much for thinking he had been pining for her.

"He was very grouchy when he left."

"He's always very grouchy."

"This was a new kind of grouchy. He's hurt, Tia," Mrs. Hernandez said, catching her hands. "I don't know what you fought about, but—"

"We didn't fight. He told me he wanted a divorce. I begged him to give things another try. He didn't want to hear it." It was finally sinking in that he really didn't want her. Not at all. Not even a little bit. She hadn't imagined everything she felt between them, but she had misjudged his reaction to it. She had been so certain she could convince him he could trust her that she'd never once considered that he didn't *want* to trust. That he didn't even want to try.

Her heart felt so heavy in her chest that Tia thought she'd faint. But rather than give in to the emotion threatening to consume her, she turned, walked to the door and grabbed her overnight case. "I guess I'll see you."

"Tia—"

"No," Tia said, taking another breath to keep herself from crumbling. "I'm fine. I knew when we got married that we'd probably divorce." Funny, but though she'd "known" it, she'd never believed it. "I'm fine."

"I'm fine!" Drew barked when Mrs. Hernandez came running out to help him with his luggage when he returned from Eleuthera the following Tuesday.

"I know that you're fine, you crusty old crab. But Miss Tia isn't."

That caused Drew's chest to tighten and his knees to weaken. "Is she sick? Is the baby okay?"

"They both seem fine."

"Then why did you say something is wrong?" he growled, more annoyed with her interfering than usual. She never stopped to consider that things might hurt him, too. No. She just pushed ahead like a damned steamroller.

"Because she came here on Friday."

"I told her not to."

"Yeah, well, sometimes she don't listen so good."

"Oh, no. No. No. No. Don't go using bad grammar on me. I know you, Mrs. H. You're smarter than anybody in this town." Except Tia, but he wouldn't let himself think about that. "You've been manipulating me since the day you got here and I'm not falling for it anymore."

"Okay, then fall for this," Mrs. Hernandez said, following him up the front porch steps. "I quit."

That made him stop. "You quit? Because I'm getting a divorce?"

She shook her head. "No. I quit because *I'm* getting married."

Drew burst out laughing, picked up his suitcase and walked across the porch. "Good one."

"I mean it," she said, catching his arm to get his attention. "I'm going back to Minneapolis."

"Back to your sister?"

"Back to the man I met while caring for my sister."

Standing on his front porch, Drew stared at his housekeeper and from the serious expression on her face, he knew she wasn't kidding. He inclined his head in the direction of the front door. "Let's go inside."

Mrs. Hernandez nodded.

Drew set his luggage in the foyer, the same way Tia had every Friday night. But he knew the placement of his bags was only part of why he thought of her the instant he stepped inside. She hadn't been in his house for days, yet the place smelled like her. He could feel her in the rooms, hear her laughter in his mind. He swallowed.

"If you'd like a little Scotch, I could get it for you," Mrs. Hernandez said, leading him into the living room.

"I'll get it myself."

"You're pretty handy with getting things for yourself."

"Which means I won't miss you," Drew shot back on his way to the bar as Mrs. Hernandez perched on the arm of the white sofa.

Mrs. Hernandez laughed. "Oh, Drew. You will miss me. You will tell yourself you don't. You will tell yourself you're strong. You'll even wash your own laundry and eat your own cooking for six weeks just to prove how strong you are. But you'll miss me."

Drew banged a glass on the bar, then reached for the Scotch bottle. "Very funny."

Mrs. Hernandez shrugged. "I guess it's a matter of perspective, because I think it's very sad."

Drew peered at her, a sudden suspicion forming in his head. "You wouldn't be doing this as a way to leave me alone so much that I miss Tia enough to ask her back?"

Mrs. Hernandez laughed. "You are the most vain man I have ever met. No, Mr. Drew. The sun does not rise and set on you. When I went to Minneapolis to care for my sister, I met a man."

He poured Scotch into the glass and, out of politeness, he offered it to her. To his surprise, she took it.

"Thanks."

Without missing a beat, Drew retrieved a second glass and Mrs. Hernandez went on. "We hit it off right away. We don't have any of the same interests, but we click." She laughed. "So, he's teaching me to play golf and I'm teaching him to play pinochle."

Drew shook his head. "I thought you said you were quitting to get married?"

"I am."

His eyes narrowed as he studied her. Finally, he said, "You're marrying a man you met six weeks ago."

She nodded. "Yes."

Frustrated, even a bit scared for the poor old woman, Drew set his drink on the bar and combed his fingers through his hair. "Okay, you and I really need to talk."

"No, we don't."

"Yes, we do! Mrs. Hernandez, it may seem that I don't like you, but I do."

She waved her hand in dismissal. "I know that."

"Then you should also realize that I'm not going to let you marry some guy you just met!"

Mrs. Hernandez laughed. "I'm almost sixty years old. You can't stop me."

He gaped at her. "You're serious."

She nodded.

"Okay, look. I'm sure your entire family has spelled out the negatives for you, but let me give this one more shot. First, it's really not very smart to marry somebody you don't know."

"You're a fine one to talk. You married Tia after one wild night after a party."

Drew's Scotch glass stopped halfway to his lips. "How do you know about that?"

She shrugged. "I have my sources."

"Who?" Drew demanded.

Mrs. Hernandez shook her head. "Not that it matters, but it was Joe," she said, referring to one of the stable hands. "Scuttlebutt got around the stable that you'd met a woman at a party you went to in Pittsburgh. It didn't take us too long to put two and two together when you announced you were getting married. Especially since Tia lives in Pittsburgh."

Drew took a breath, realizing he had been correct. She *had* been suspicious. Not because of Elizabeth, but she had been suspicious.

"I thought it was good that you married Tia," Mrs. Hernandez continued, "because it proves that deep down inside you're a good man. But it doesn't change the fact that you married someone you barely know."

"Which is exactly my point! Look how that turned out. In case you missed the memo, we're getting a divorce."

"I won't be so stubborn, and neither will Nolan."

Drew sighed. "Tia and I aren't stubborn."

"You're right. Tia isn't stubborn, but you are. And I'm not. And neither is Nolan."

"No matter how good your intentions, things may not work out."

"I disagree. I think things will work out because I will make sure they work out."

"And what if he decides otherwise?"

"He won't."

Drew persisted. "What if he does? Or better yet… You're no spring chicken. I'm guessing Nolan isn't, either. What if he dies? What will you do then?"

"Then I will have memories."

"Baloney."

"Baloney, yourself! How do you think I would feel if he really did die and I let time go by without spending it with him? I'd be devastated." She rose from the sofa arm and set her Scotch glass on the coffee table. "Even if we have only two weeks, it will be two wonderful weeks because I will make the best of every damned day."

She stood directly in front of the bar and held Drew's gaze. "You may not care if you waste your life one day at a time and lock out anybody who might be foolish enough to love you, but I'm not so stupid." She paused and tilted her head. "Or maybe it's because I've seen how stupid you've been with Tia that I won't let my opportunity pass me by. Even if I only have two weeks, I want them. Goodbye, Mr. Drew. I was going to work out a two-week notice, but now I know I need to leave immediately because you're right. None of us knows how much time we have with the person we love and unlike you, I refuse to waste a second of mine."

She left the room and just as she'd said, she packed her bags and was gone within an hour. Drew stared after her as she drove her little blue car off his property.

He wasn't angry with her. He felt a little silly for actually talking her into going when he was trying to talk her into staying, but deep down inside he was pulling for her.

He wished for her sake that she was right. That she would have the memories of her time together with this man she thought she loved.

But whether she knew it or not she had actually hit Drew and Tia's problem on the head. They had too much time. Years to hurt each other. Years to leave each other.

He simply couldn't risk it.

Chapter Eleven

Lightning streaked across the sky as Tia drove toward her parents' farm. Since leaving Pittsburgh almost eight hours before, the farther south she went, the stronger the storm had become. And the stronger the storm had become, the slower she drove and the tighter her nerves stretched. She had a sneaking suspicion she was heading into the remnants of the hurricane she'd heard her coworkers discussing, but she didn't know for sure. She hadn't had time to listen to the radio or watch the Weather Channel. She hadn't had time for anything but work. Which was why she had decided to come home this weekend. She couldn't tell her parents about her dead marriage in a phone conversation. She knew from the calls she'd had with them these past two weeks that Drew hadn't told them. But that was fine. They were *her* parents. She should be the one to tell them that she and Drew were not staying married.

Lightning again crackled through the darkness. Rain beat against Tia's windshield. Her wipers could barely keep her vision clear. Wind buffeted her little car. She approached Drew's farm and—stiff from holding the steering wheel so tightly and scared silly—she darned near stopped, but didn't. Not because of pride, but because she knew she couldn't take the look on his face when he saw her. Even if she explained that she only wanted to get out of the rain, he'd think she was trying to manipulate him.

She understood why he was skeptical; he didn't trust. He couldn't. She'd naively believed that once he got to know her he would trust her. But he didn't. She'd let herself be vulnerable, opened up to him, given him everything she had and he still didn't trust her. Instead, when they got to the point where he needed to make a choice, he'd decided to hurt her. And that was the most telling thing of all. Rather than take the step he'd so desperately wanted to take and risk being hurt himself, he'd hurt her.

So, after hours of maneuvering her little sports car over rain-slicked roads, dodging puddles and steering against the wind, she didn't wish to endure a scene. She didn't want to see the suspicious look on his face. Worse, she didn't want to soften in her feelings toward him because she knew that deep down inside he was hurting. She didn't want to feel compassion. Didn't want to understand him. Didn't want to ache for him.

She simply wanted shelter. Happy shelter. Somewhere everybody would be glad to see her. She didn't want to hurt anymore.

So she passed the lane to Drew's farm, deciding to risk another ten minutes on the road. After all, she'd driven this far. Now that she was on the less-traveled country road she could easily get herself to her parents' in one piece. She wouldn't bother Drew. She knew it hurt him to hurt her. She didn't want to understand, but she did. And that was what was killing her. Because she understood, she couldn't even try to change his mind. She knew better.

When she was just a few yards past Drew's lane, the entire world around her lit up. A crack of thunder accompanied the lightning, meaning the strike had been nearby. As quickly as Tia concluded that, a tree fell on the road in front of her.

She swerved to miss it, but overcompensated and her tires spun on the roadside gravel, sending her car careening out of control. The steering wheel spun so fast and so hard, Tia thought it would rip her arms out of their sockets as it wrenched itself out of her hold. Without having the steering wheel to anchor her, she bounced backward, then forward, hitting her head hard enough that the world instantly blackened.

Dressed in a slicker and cursing a blue streak, Drew ventured out into the rain. He couldn't believe someone had left on a light in the barn, but even through the wall of rain he could see the glow. He slammed the door behind him and huddled inside his rain gear against the driving rain, but only two feet off his porch he realized the light wasn't in his barn. What he was seeing were car headlights and they were coming from a small strip of land he hadn't cleared but had left as a wetland because a creek ran through it.

Realizing the person inside the car could be hurt, Drew forgot about protecting himself from the rain and ran toward the wrecked vehicle. Rain pummeled his head and shoulders. His boots were ensnared in sticky mud several times, but he yanked them out and kept running. About fifty feet away from the car, he realized it was small and red. About ten feet after that he recognized it as Tia's.

His heart stopped but his legs grew stronger. He raced to her car and to his relief, he could open the door, but when he leaned inside, he not only saw Tia was out cold, he also saw a cut on her head. Blood poured down her face.

As rain beat against his back, he patted his shirt pocket for his cell phone but it wasn't there. Reaching over Tia, he grabbed her purse and found her cell.

He quickly dialed Ben's number and when Elizabeth answered, he said, "Call an ambulance." The wind picked up. Rain pounded around him. To be heard above the noise, he shouted, "Tia wrecked her car. She's in a ditch right off the main road in front of my lane. Hurry."

With that, he disconnected the call and bent inside her car again. "Tia?" He wasn't sure if it was right or wrong to wake her. He only remembered advice about not letting people with a concussion sleep and he reached in and shook her shoulder slightly. "Tia. Wake up."

She didn't move, and fear gripped Drew. He pressed two fingers against her neck and found a pulse but it was weak. She was bleeding so fast he didn't have a clue how to stop it and what she had of a pulse slowed under his fingers.

He unexpectedly remembered what Mrs. Hernandez had said the week before about not wasting time and he realized that was all he had done. Waste time. He'd found somebody he liked. Somebody who liked him, and instead of rejoicing he'd been an idiot. Bossing her. Mistrusting her. Almost accusing her of trying to trick him when she'd first told him she was pregnant. Then kicking her out of his life for good.

And now she might die. And their baby might die. And everything he'd almost had would slip through his fingers again. Only this time, he would deserve it.

He pulled out of the car and lifted his face to the rain, screaming his frustration into the wind. Why couldn't he trust? Why couldn't he get beyond the fear of being hurt?

He patted down his shirt pocket again and this time found what he was looking for. The sonogram picture. His hope for a future. He'd stared at this a hundred times, memorized the shadowy lines, sometimes hoping it really was a girl, other times hoping he would have a son. In the two weeks since he'd forced Tia away, he had clung to this picture as a lifeline because he believed one child would be enough. Now, he suddenly knew one child wasn't enough to build a life. He wanted the baby's mother. He *wanted* her. He wanted to love her and take care of her and argue with her and just plain have fun with her.

She couldn't die. Their baby couldn't die. He wouldn't let them.

He reached into the car again. At the same time he heard the wail of the ambulance siren as it pierced through the noise of the storm.

"Tia. Wake up."

Her breathing shifted and he hoped that meant she had heard him, but she didn't stir, didn't awaken and he feared the shift in her breathing might not have been good. Listening more closely, he recognized she was now gasping for breath.

"Tia! You have to wake up!" Panic gripped him so hard his heart actually hurt. He couldn't believe she was going to die, that he was going to lose her for good. But he was.

Tears swelled painfully in his eyes. He dropped his forehead to her chest. "Tia. Tia," he whispered. "Don't die. Please, don't die."

"Drew?" She said his name slowly, her voice coming thick and sluggish and on a wheeze of breath.

"Yes!" He straightened away from her and his gaze jumped to her face. "It's me. I'm here."

"I'm sorry."

"You have nothing to be sorry for," he said, studying her. Her eyes hadn't opened. She could barely move her mouth. And there wasn't a damned thing he could do to help her. All he could do was wait. He pushed her bangs away from her wound.

"Don't want to bother you. Don't want to make you mad."

"You're not a bother," he said, but her words hit him like an arrow in the heart. She was the best thing that had ever happened to him and he'd made her feel that she was a bother.

"Tried to make it to my mother's. A tree fell."

"It's okay," he said softly as the ambulance crew began running the short distance from the road where they'd parked.

"It's okay," he repeated, trailing his fingers across her forehead, again nudging her hair away from her cut.

"No. It's not okay. You like your privacy. I won't ever bother you again."

This time a new feeling skittered through Drew. He wasn't even sure what to name it. She'd debated stopping at his house to get out of the storm, but she'd changed her mind because she knew he didn't want to be bothered.

Had he done the ultimate damage? Had he pushed her so far that she no longer saw any good in him? Had she come to her senses the way he'd been directing her to, and now she wanted nothing to do with him?

Aaron Felix shoved him out of the way. "Move, Drew!" he said, yelling to be heard above the rain.

Drew stepped back. A few seconds later Ben's truck skidded to a stop behind the ambulance. Elizabeth and Ben jumped out. They didn't even approach Drew. And why should they? By now, Tia had probably told them he'd asked for a divorce. By now they knew he'd hurt

Tia. It was more proof that he'd blown it. Totally. There would be no second chance for him.

Ben and Elizabeth ran to Aaron. "Is she okay?" Ben yelled.

Aaron answered, but Drew didn't hear. Edging away, he took an additional step back. Then another. Then another. All this time he'd blamed Sandy for ruining his ability to trust, but he now knew the choice had been his. And he'd chosen wrong. If Tia wanted nothing to do with him, he deserved it.

Eventually, he turned and headed to his house. Nobody even noticed he had gone.

Two days later Tia was sitting up in her hospital bed laughing with Marian and Lily. The fifty-something divorcée and twenty-two-year-old graphic artist had little in common, but for some reason or another it didn't matter. Marian mothered Lily and Lily—with her vast experience of six months on an ad team—mentored Marian. The pair simply made Tia laugh.

"So, Lou decides the best thing to do with Mr. Barrington is to use humor," Marian said.

When she paused, Lily eagerly picked up the story. "And he goes to his mother's house and borrows one of her suits. It was an old brown one that actually looks a lot like a really ugly one you wear when you're trying to look older. Anyway, then he buys a dark brown wig and dresses like you for the presentation."

"Are you kidding?" Tia said, then she gasped. "He didn't!"

"He did," Marian continued as Lily leaned out the door, Tia suspected, to make sure a nurse wasn't on her way to tell them to keep down the noise. "He walked in, big as life, wearing that suit and wig, without shaving his moustache or legs, and he said, 'Good morning, I'm Tia Capriotti and I'm here to give my presentation on the Barrington Cereal account.'"

"What did Mr. Holden say?" Tia said, through gasping laughs as she pictured Lou in his mother's brown suit, wearing a wig.

"He said, 'Sit down, Lou.' And Lou said, 'No. Today, I'm not Lou. Today I'm Tia because most of this campaign is her idea and she deserves the credit.'"

Tia stopped laughing. "Are you kidding?"

Marian smiled. "No. He wanted you to get credit."

"That's so sweet."

"Speaking of sweet," Lily said, "your husband is walking down the hall."

Tia grabbed Marian's hand. Working late one night, Tia had admitted to Marian that her marriage wasn't just over, it was a sham. Marian had offered her the good advice of accepting Drew's decision to divorce and move on. Tia hadn't exactly felt better, but at least she knew she was doing the right thing. But she hadn't expected to ever have to speak with him again.

"Oh, no."

"Hey," Marian said. "You can do this."

Tia shook her head. "I don't think so. The guy hates me and instead of staying the heck away from him, I wrecked my car in his front yard."

"You'll be fine," Lily said before she bent down and hugged Tia. "We'll see you later."

Tia shot an imploring glance at Marian, who shook her head no and slipped out of the room ten seconds before Drew walked in.

Tia pretended great interest in her TV, then glanced over as if only noticing him. Wanting to get this visit over with as quickly as possible, she casually said, "Hey. Hi, Drew." She didn't want him to think she was pining. She most definitely didn't want him to think she needed him. She wanted him gone, so she could get over loving a man whom she had done nothing but annoy for the past several weeks.

"Hi." He thrust the roses at her. "I brought you these."

"Thanks," she said, trying to sound casual, but feeling her voice weakening. Not only did he look wonderful, but he'd also brought her flowers. Of course, he probably felt compelled since she was the mother of his child. Nine chances out of ten he was here to make sure everything was fine with the baby. She needed to remember that.

"There's a water pitcher around here somewhere…" She turned on her side and began to edge out of the bed, but Drew stopped her by grabbing her upper arm.

"Don't."

Not able to look at him when he was this close and touching her, she shifted away, waving her free hand in dismissal. "I can walk. I'm fine. A little concussion. The doctor said I should be out of here tomorrow."

Still holding her arm, Drew gently eased her back to the bed. "I know. I called."

But he hadn't come. He hadn't even come to the emergency room. That was when she'd had to explain the truth about her marriage to her parents.

He busied himself with finding the water pitcher, but when he did it was too small for the flowers.

Tia said, "Don't worry about them. I'll have my mother bring a vase."

"That would be great."

"Yeah." She fiddled with the covers. "So, since you called, you also know everything's fine with the baby."

He nodded.

"All rightie, then," she said, smiling up at him, trying to force a happiness she didn't feel because she just wanted him out of her room. He didn't love her. She was a fool to love him. She wanted to get on with the rest of her life.

"So, we're great. Everything's great. And your responsibility here is done. You can go."

He swallowed, but otherwise didn't move.

"Really," she said, smiling again. "You can go."

"Are you saying that because you're trying to make my life easier, or are you saying that because you really want me to go?"

Tia almost sighed. Nothing was ever simple with this guy. "A little bit of both, I guess."

"And I know I deserve that."

This time Tia did sigh. "You don't deserve anything, Drew. We made a mistake. We tried to fix it by getting married. It worked fine to save my dad from being over-stressed and not so well from other perspectives. But there's no need for a debriefing. Let's just move on."

"Is that what you want?"

She sighed again, but this time she looked at him. "What difference does it make?"

"It makes a lot of difference."

"Why? So you can get all righteously indignant with me and tell me again how you can't trust?"

"No, because I do trust you. And, the other day, when I was waiting for the ambulance I realized that Mrs. Hernandez was right."

She stared at him. "Mrs. Hernandez?"

"Yeah."

"You never think she's right."

He shrugged. "Usually she isn't, but she left me, too."

Tia gaped at him. "You ran off your housekeeper?"

"No, she left me to get married. While she was caring for her sister, she met a man. Apparently, it was love at first sight. She was going to work out a notice, but somehow or another I talked her into realizing life was short and she needed to have every minute she could get with this guy…Nolan."

Tia took a second to digest what he'd said, then she laughed her first real laugh in weeks. "Well, isn't that great!"

"I got a postcard. She's very happy."

Tia shook her head in wonder. "Wow."

"But before she left, she yelled at me."

"She was always yelling at you."

"This time she told me I was an idiot and I agreed."

Not quite sure how to reply to that, Tia said nothing.

"When I cautioned her about marrying a guy she'd just met, she countered that I was an idiot who never took advantage of good things when I had them." He paused and met her gaze. "I realized how right she was when I stood there helplessly, watching you out cold in your car, not sure how injured you were."

"I'm fine," Tia whispered.

He drew a long breath. "I know. That's kind of why I'm here. I don't want to waste any more time."

Holding her breath, Tia didn't reply. She knew this was hard for him, but if he was taking them to the point she thought he might be taking them, he had to say it. All of it. Every darned word. She wasn't assuming anything anymore.

"I would like to be married for real."

She wanted to leap into his arms. Instead, she forced herself not to speak because he still hadn't said what she needed to hear.

He pulled in a breath. "No comment on that?"

"I'm not a hundred percent sure what you're saying."

"I'm saying I want to be married to you…forever." He caught her gaze. "For real."

She shook her head. "It's not enough."

He gaped at her. "Not enough? What do you want from a guy who fell in love with you in four weeks of weekends?"

Tia flopped back against her pillow. *That* was what she wanted to hear. She took a breath, then another, then she said, "Say it again."

"What?"

"Don't play stupid cowboy with me. Say it again."

"I love you."

"Again."

His lips twitched. "I love you."

"Again."

He burst out laughing. "No! Damn it! I said it. I meant it. Just like you said, it's time to move on."

For that, Tia scrambled up in bed and all but flung herself into his arms. "That's the guy I love."

"You like me grouchy?"

"I like you as the real you. Deep down inside you're good. And you know what? I'm keeping you."

"You damned well better," he said, then kissed her soundly. "Because I got the estimate on your car. It's totaled. If we're staying married, I'll buy you another."

Tia melted against him, holding on to him tightly, afraid she was dreaming, even though she knew she wasn't. "I already said I was keeping you."

"Then you've got yourself another red sports car."

"All right! And since you're willing to buy me a car, I'll compromise, too."

He frowned. "What have you got to barter?"

"My job."

"You can't give up your job."

Tia smiled. "No, but I could begin working from home. We'll try it in the last few months of my pregnancy and see if it works out." Unable to resist, she kissed him again.

But when she attempted to pull away, this time it was Drew who clung to her. "I'm so sorry. I didn't mean to hurt you. I didn't want to be afraid."

Tia shifted out of his embrace. "Hey, cowboys don't get scared. You weren't scared, you were cautious."

He burst out laughing. "Right."

"And that's the story we'll tell our kids when they're old enough to hear."

At the mention of their kids, he flattened his hand on her stomach, then looked into her eyes. "Are you sure you're okay?"

"Positive."

How could she not be okay? She was married to the man of her dreams, had a baby on the way and was about to get a new sports car.

Life did not get any better than this, and just as she'd thought the day she'd run into him at the party, this really was her lucky year.

* * * * *

Hidden in the secrets of antiquity, lies the unimagined truth...

Introducing

a brand-new line filled with mystery and suspense, action and adventure, and a fascinating look into history.

And it all begins with DESTINY.

In a sealed crypt in France, where the terrifying legend of the beast of Gevaudan begins to unravel, Annja Creed discovers a stunning artifact that will seal her destiny.

Available every other month starting July 2006, wherever you buy books.

**Four sisters.
A family legacy.
And someone is out to destroy it.**

A captivating new limited continuity, launching June 2006

The most beautiful hotel in New Orleans,
and someone is out to destroy it. But mystery,
danger and some surprising family revelations
and discoveries won't stop the Marchand sisters
from protecting their birthright...
and finding love along the way.

Page-turning drama…

Exotic, glamorous locations…

Intense emotion and passionate seduction…

Sheikhs, princes and billionaire tycoons…

This summer, may we suggest:

THE SHEIKH'S DISOBEDIENT BRIDE
by Jane Porter
On sale June.

AT THE GREEK TYCOON'S BIDDING
by Cathy Williams
On sale July.

THE ITALIAN MILLIONAIRE'S VIRGIN WIFE
On sale August.

With new titles to choose from every month, discover a world of romance in our books written by internationally bestselling authors.

SILHOUETTE *Romance*®

COMING NEXT MONTH

#1822 PRICELESS GIFTS—Cara Colter
A Father's Wish
Sure her father is trying to keep her safe from some crazed stalker,
but firing her staff and removing her from her luxury suite to her
crazy aunt's farm is going too far! Chelsea King is pretty sure the
situation can't get any worse—until she meets her new bodyguard,
Randall Peabody. An ex-soldier—broken, scarred, protective—
Randall stirs something in Chelsea and makes her feel as if she
hasn't really lived until now....

#1823 THE BRIDE'S BEST MAN—Judy Christenberry
Logic and order are Shelby Cook's typical, lawyerly methods. But
when she goes with her aunt on a much-needed vacation to Hawaii,
she never expects to meet her long-lost father and to be attracted to
his friend Pete Campbell. Shelby doesn't think the attraction will
go anywhere, but Pete is about to show her that true love defies all
limitations and logic!

#1824 ONE MAN AND A BABY—Susan Meier
The Cupid Campaign
Experience has taught Ashley Meljac not to trust her instincts
regarding men, especially when it comes to the town's resident bad
boy—Rick Capriotti. Still, something in the way he cares for his
baby makes her forget the past and dream about a future with him
and his adorable toddler....

#1825 HERE WITH ME—Holly Jacobs
After divorce and a miscarriage, Lee Singer just craves quiet and
solitude. But soon Adam Benton, a workaholic with a one-year-old
in tow, arrives back in town. And all too soon he's brought noise and
life to her world and got her questioning what she truly desires.

SRCNM0606